PRISONERS
OF
DESIRE

PRISONERS OF DESIRE

A Novel

David Orsini

PRISONERS OF DESIRE

Copyright © 2024 by David Orsini
First Edition Quaternity™ Books 2024
Quaternity™ Books
ISBN 978-1-943691-48-7
Cover Design by James Buchanan

Other Books by David Orsini

The Price of Happiness
The Enchantments
The Reappearing
The Weaver of Plots
Schemes, Disguises, & Traps
Vanishing by Degrees
The Ghost Lovers
The Woman Who Loved Too Well
The Subtleties of Seduction
Bitterness / Seven Stories

CONTENTS

"That which we call sin in others is experiment for us."
--Ralph Waldo Emerson,
"Experience," *Essays: Second Series*

"Be sure of this: your sin will find you out."
--*Holy Bible*, Numbers, Chapter 32, Verse 23

"We are punished by our sins, not for them."
--Elbert Hubbard, *The Notebook of Elbert Hubbard*

PART ONE

THE SUBTLETIES OF SEDUCTION

1

The morning after her father and Malcolm Turner had arranged things so that there would be no scandal, Linda Maguire awoke feeling uneasy. She had every right to believe that she had been betrayed. She had allowed herself, perhaps as a way of easing her sister Tracy's grief over the recent death of their mother, to be caught up in a most awkward situation. The entire incident had been tinted with the moral ambiguities that she abhorred and that, she'd believed, her parents had influenced their daughters to abhor.

Casting its shadow upon them all, the episode had occurred within an extended July visit to the home of her fiancé Steven's parents, Daniel and Olivia Bradford. She, her father, and her sister had been enjoying an agreeable month of summery activities radiating from the Bradfords' superb estate in Newport, Rhode Island, while her father's own splendid home a mile away on Ocean Drive was being revised by a team of architects, landscapers, and interior designers. Within the four weeks of their visit in midsummer 1920, Daniel and Olivia had provided them with every resource of their hospitality that might allay the sorrow that had not left them even six months after her mother's death.

During what was for them an essential season of adjustment, she and her sister joined a small sailing party that included her always admirable Steven. In addition, there was Ryan Turner. Although he appeared to be a Harvard friend of the Bradfords' younger son, Aaron, he made himself far more available to almost every other young person within convenient miles of the Bradfords' imposing seaside property.

Ryan was a descendant of eminent Turners who had amassed their first fortunes in shipbuilding centuries earlier. Later they had amassed a profusion of more immense fortunes in iron, oil, and steel while acquiring the status of the legendary because of heroic exploits not only in various wars, but also in law and government. With careless assurance, he had drawn her eighteen-year-old sister into an ambiguous episode that might have compromised her. That this same Ryan Turner belonged to a family that had, through so many momentous ordeals and the most grievous personal tragedies, always maintained its obligations to the highest ethical standard, only made his wild youth's indiscretions that much more dismaying. Although he was an assertive young man nearly twenty and well-trained surely in the code of behavior that men of his class were expected to represent dutifully and instantaneously (he was, after all, Malcolm Turner's son), he did not always do his part. Too often, his actions were, if not wrong in their intention, certainly ambivalent in their resolution. By so behaving, he cast a cloud upon those friends whom he persuaded to join him in his adventures.

Yet there was something altogether appealing about the imaginative ways in which he tested himself and tested others, as well. Linda found herself still liking him because of his restless and creative approach to the world. Besides, although he had initiated the wayward trajectory of those hours, he was not the only person responsible for everything that went wrong that afternoon.

During one of the Bradfords' magnificent Sundays, Ryan casually suggested that they—Steven with her in his new, rugged yawl, and Ryan alone in his sailboat—should race against each other in winds far more vigorous than those which allowed them their recent victory in a regatta. The day was warm, with pearl-gray clouds scattering toward the horizon. The wind made the air occasionally aggressive, its heat more sullen, more palpably moist and no longer comforting.

After the day's casual rhythms betrayed their expectations, Steven's and hers, she remembered that Ryan had persuaded them to leave imperceptibly the Bradfords' grand summer party. By so persuading, he had led them to a path that compromised her sister's reputation. Unpredictable and mysterious Ryan was—with swagger so carelessly self-reliant that you believed at once the hard-bodied lankiness possessing it would treat both happiness and hardship with equal indifference. Clever and intriguing as well, he had captivated Steven and her in this first summer of their feeling they belonged to one another, though they were not yet married. He had captivated them completely, her usually reserved yet always creditable Steven and her as well, through the sheer splendor of seeing him, a vigorous youth of their class, react with such easy and spontaneous freedom to possibility's ambivalent turnings. Though several years younger than Steven and without his brutal experience of the war, he was in many ways just as knowing, just as canny about the world's bruising, addictive textures.

Subtly and plausibly, he had drawn them away from the bountiful array of banquet tables with sun-gold canopies. There, in the midst of a wide expanse of greenery, visiting ambassadors and moguls, poets and scientists, and artists and philosophers mingled with crisp assurance, glad to share their hosts' ornate repast and their own animated convictions. He had led them to an enshadowed grove of lilac trees—white, lavender and crimson.

When they had arrived at the entrance to the grove, she noticed the glowing red border of berberis and verbena and amaranthus with velvety spikes stirring as if wakened to the proximities of blue agapanthus and plum-purple hollyhock and white lavaterra which were swaying at the side of silver grasses. She noticed, too, as she glanced inside the grove, how the recessions of light-reflected shadows overtook the vigorous ripple of tree colors there, disguising essential definitions of color and distance, too, so that space—welling backwards—darkened and disappeared within rising layers of dusk.

Everything about that day, in her retrospection at least, appeared disguised or dislocated. Even the wind seemed something other than itself. For when they'd paused on the emerald-rich hill leading to the sinuous path of the grove, she had believed just for an instant that the summery wind was the purest music, a melodious ornament of the air. Yet it was not the wind at all that she had heard or, rather, not the wind alone. She'd had to turn 'round, though, to discover the true-seeming source of the sound, allowing her gaze to move back to the banquet tables and sun-tinted people and back to festive images flowing in and out of the day's nebulous margins. Then, beyond those images, she saw once more the southwest corner of the Bradfords' main house. Its elegant Tudor ambiance wore exquisite shell carving along the gable trim, basketweave-and herringbone-patterned brick, and diamond-motif leaded windows. In that corner exuberant musicians orchestrated the convivial voices and self-reflective conversations of the guests (still sauntering along the banquet greenery) with the more mellifluous intonations of piano and violin, oboe and piccolo, trumpet and clarinet and tuba.

It was that confluence of sounds she had heard. The meld of resonating music and moody wind and pulsing human voices influenced—indeed, disguised—everything that she heard. Nothing was as it was alone. Each swelling timbre appropriated vibrancies other than its own and became something apart from and more than itself, concealed as it was within the melody of the wind and the hum of human voices and the lyrical harmonies of music.

From her implicated senses the day suppressed its accuracies, offering to her inquiring attention sights and sounds merely oblique in their truths, as if their essential reality were shunning the deepest layers of her comprehension. For the colors of the leaves were blemished by shadows in the grove. The music from the terrace was more than itself alone. Human voices floated inside soft cadences of wind. White, spumy waves tossed fitfully on the gentle-seeming ocean that flowed with glimmering ease below the hill where then she stood. And, here before her, Ryan Turner's laughing innocence flickered and gleamed like a temporary sun on the sea and just as quickly vanished. Yet each of these emblems of the day, these flourishing experiences of her senses, claimed a plausibility and justified an acceptance of the outward appearance of things.

With quiet confidence she had quickly accepted the outward appearance of things—all the palpable images of the iridescent earth and the suddenly flamingo clouds and the Prussian blue sea that had not yet reconciled themselves to the languorous drift of haze come to cover whole curvatures of space. Nor had she regarded as anything more than casual suggestion Ryan's apparently spontaneous remark that they—she and Steven—might enjoy standing upon the very promontory that had inspired the opening passages of the latest poem in a cycle which he had, for a year now, been composing.

They accepted his invitation because perhaps they wanted to retire discreetly, though only momentarily, from the gregarious fervor of that immense afternoon. Or possibly their furtive need for the unexpected persuaded them to join him. Or, more likely, their healthy pleasure in being drawn to the threshold of a young poet's imagination influenced them to peer for an instant upon the sensuous nature of his vision. His writerly skill enabled him to re-create the configurations of inlet and bay, grove and greenscape, festive sounds and flowered scents.

That Ryan Turner chose to express in poetic lines the vigorous narrative that was his life gave her soul-quickening pleasure. She had learned through wide travels with her parents and tutors and through voluminous reading in philosophy and history to associate authentic men, those charismatic ones who left their own firm imprints on the lacerating, rugged world, with keen-edged literary minds and self-willed heroic prowess. Her studies had, in fact, taught her to admire the youthful exuberance of Wordsworth in Paris scanning a momentous revolution, the burning wildness of Byron crying out to freedom at Missalonghi, and the prodigious Wilfred Owen daring to confront the stark blank sky at the Sambre Canal, knowing full well he had come to the end of the world.

To observe Ryan Turner whole and undiminished, his golden muscularity a summer radiance roused and compelling, was (she told herself) to witness manly assurance on the brink of new heroism and to recall once again the swiftly lived glories of those proven-brave poets. Whether he, too, would feel calm and original after the cleansing hour of rebellion or, risking all on a self-consuming deed, climb over the dark rim into early death, his steady eyes glazed in a face gone still and seraphic, only leavening time would finally disclose. But here, within the *now* that was this warm dissolving day, he seemed by himself alone a vivid justification for passion-wrought humanness.

"I want to find the hidden essence of things and of

people," he told them confidently, as though confidence were the husky membrane of his potency. "There's adventure in that."

He had been explaining why, with its secret-furling winds and slanted whorls of light and shadows spun like wheels covering alcoves that surprised, he had chosen for the vista at the threshold of his poem a stalwart promontory which appeared to possess in full the summer-fragrant grove stirring behind it. In his eyes the promontory stood apparently indomitable while it waited for the sometimes-eddying sky and the dark, reeling waves of a storm-riven bay.

"This, I tell you, is a place where adventure should begin."

He held them carefully, Steven and even more so herself, inside that penetrating look of his that pulsed at the edge of what she regarded as a playful beckoning toward near-wildness. It was his promise of the unexpected and the surprise of her liking him so intensely which first put her off her proper course.

Yet even then, just before the festive afternoon wambled and tilted and whirled away from her control, she still consented to him as he dared her to thread her way unbaffled through his rapid processes. In that hour, while her heart toward him satisfied still with its gathering fullness, she had felt a tighter breathing rising fast from an unnoticed corner of her soul. This throbbing exhilaration he was drawing out of her was unanticipated evidence that in her especially there lived a splendid array of differences she had not yet tested, though they were so much more than the difference that was her safe demureness.

So it was that he had persuaded her (as if he were there alone beside her, murmuring his approval) to parry in a playful mode his spirited remark that the rugged promontory (where flashes of the dissolving afternoon sun vibrated like vaporous silver and where with them in seeming-casualness he stood) was an inspired place for finding a solid adventure. Before parrying his remark, she moved closer to Steven to clasp his large, athletic hands over the delicate touch of her own, so that all that she in that moment did or said seemed married to him alone. Only then did she speak the words that made her feel, in a rushing instant of newness, replenished and enlightened.

"We'll make an adventure for you, if you can't find one already here."

She saw at once that her brisk words awakened their keener awareness—her reliable Steven's, all earnest response and openness, and the far more complicated Ryan's, engendered as it was by his finely measured ambiguity. Through a language of hands answering the appealing promise of her vivid declaration, Steven clasped her ardently, as if this fluent motion of hands might leave upon her skin a permanent imprint of his heated body. But it was Ryan who gamely tossed her way the confident reply which called out to her desire to make an adventure.

"Feel free," he smoothly told her, his full, sensual lips once more in teasing union with a smile. His blue eyes were studying the hint of elation in her blue eyes and in her titian-haired refinement. That afternoon his resonating voice offered what she had accepted as a playful invitation. Hours later she would recognize it as the insidious challenge he had meant it to be—and he hardened and unflinching before the recoil of his words.

Now, in the press of desires no longer quiescent within her, his words were like wiry tendrils fastening their hold upon the secret senses inside her flesh, and not only his words, but his whole compelling presence. She accepted him entirely. She accepted, that is, the throbbing pulse of life he represented. While he was there all manly prowess before her, she seemed alone with him and complete in the sweep and push of that dissolving moment. Without waiting to feel herself lifted higher on the flow and arc of his tantalizing nearness or to ply him once more with witty retort or to attend the marrow and husk of her faithful Steven's briskness, she had to turn spontaneously and obliquely toward a remoter, far more steadying vision, her way of reclaiming a milder ease.

What she saw within the opaque-blue furling of

distance, what directed her gaze to the floating pastel sky, was the umber ripple of a stray herring gull curving the dark flash of its wings against the tumescence of ponderous clouds. After an instant's pause, it plummeted with wily skill to the consenting lips of ocean water, the better to pluck for its meal a raw, ample fish or a tiny, mackerel-tinted seabird.

Though the vision gave her back what she had not sought, the imagery of danger shown natural and beautiful, she grasped comfortably its familiar message and found again her realistic measure for understanding things. Turning once more, still toward the east, she was not surprised to sight the zinc-white hang of wind-bleached cliffs glaring like the sea-tossed bones of a devoured world. She noticed, too, across and above quick Atlantic waters and on the crest of sun-glanced fertile hills—right there, at the wavering margins of the nebulous woods—a gray-blue immensity of swaying larches that apparently grew into the sky and, before her calmer eyes, joined all of heaven's restless and eerie motion.

She turned yet again, back to inspired and risk-taking Ryan standing before her and back to her essential Steven. Having so nearly reclaimed her composure, she could now permit herself to accept with concealed joy the full-bodied danger of Ryan's sensuality. Turning, she found once more what, despite her wakened need, she had not expected: the loop and list and swell of real adventure, like a dark, risen wave pitching upon them. This reckless Ryan and her rugged Steven, in extemporaneous league or seeming so, had devised a swaggering test of unbridled courage. They'd drawn up and sealed their casual pact in the brief moments she had looked away from their virile emphasis to reflect upon the wily laws of a hovering gull and the sea-anchored gravity of sullen, white cliffs and the arrogant powers of giant, majestic larches.

Their daring plan seemed to belong to both of them, so compatible with Ryan did Steven's sudden inclination toward risk make him. Yet it was Ryan, she surmised, who had first expressed the thought that, playful and unyielding, they should ride the wind-raked swell of the sea to test their fiercer capacities. During the previous week's lively regatta, they had harnessed to the spirals of their own mastery the summer water's more temperate powers. That was a compelling reason to push themselves beyond the tight strictures of the ordinary. Racing against that afternoon's imminence of storm, they would confront with laughing camaraderie the sea's arduous, tangled restlessness. Or so, she learned upon turning back to them, Ryan had casually suggested. The even timbre of his affable words (she imagined later) modulated like sun-flecked shadows the glare of his hardened carelessness.

Their aim, he quickly explained once she had turned

back to them, was to bring Steven's new, streamlined yawl into the afternoon's uneasy waters. Its vibrant-swift force would be poised against the sturdy, proven craft that Ryan intended to navigate. If the local Coast Guard station had issued prompt warning of the weather's uncertain temperament, that was not sufficient cause, Ryan said, for postponing what promised to be a lively competition. The race would be a realistic calculation of their seamanship and of the stamina of the boats whose speed they would command.

Call the experience an exhilarating complement to the day's festive atmosphere, he suggested, or a confident summoning of the courage required for a rapid skirmish with the sea or, perhaps, their conscious shaping of an episode worth the telling in his poem. Call it, they must, as they liked, he shrugged before both of them now, moments after she had turned back to them. But they should not, through a habit of safer propensities, forfeit the pulsing capacity they held within themselves—each of them—for venturing bravely into the immense world's shifting possibilities.

Ryan spoke as if for all of them. Yet she understood at once that his words, a brisk way to glance at self-defeating reticence, were meant for her alone. For long ago, she suspected, he had left behind with laughing disdain the hesitation which stymies or trammels brave-hearted enterprise. In these few weeks of their knowing him, he had already witnessed Steven's capacity to confront the unknown without the circumspection that too cautiously measures probability, the over-refined analysis that diminishes or deflects both force and originality. Sailing in a formidable regatta, he and Steven together had winningly demonstrated the symmetry and sweep of authentic daring. So it was she toward whom he had just then directed the vigor and shape of his words.

Because, perhaps, he meant to validate her intuition, he held her firmly, as though they alone were there together, within the throb and tension of his gaze.

"You're joining us, of course," he told her. His self-assurance generated quite naturally the coiling rhythms into which he was drawing her.

If she paused, it was only for an instant, to tally the cost to her safe ease of his startling invitation. Then, casting aside all her familiar reckonings and most of her misgivings, she accepted the freefall into his challenge.

"What a grand idea," she found herself saying. The sheer pleasure of being in dangerous flight with him was new and exotic.

But no sooner had she done so, no sooner had she entered without open chute or ballast of any other kind the thrilling plunge into all that he was offering her, than she looked with delicate inquiry toward Steven. It had become her habit to interpret through his studious eyes her subtle effect upon a scene. How often she had sought out and found among a mingling concourse of guests and during their brightest repartee his beaming consent to whatever words or gestures she had chosen for that moment to define herself. She had sought out, as well, amidst graver matters, when she in his presence was able to stand reliably alone before the lacerating betrayals of a day's serener promises, his quiet approval that held at bay the show of every response except civility.

Today, though, when the stillness that held Steven's features tight came now to watch with him her curious alterations, he offered her neither consent nor dismay. His was the courtesy which quietly beholds the different tint or sudden, complicated traceries of a young woman's character. So long, or so it seemed, did he pause inside his stillness, so fraught with anticipation did he render her art of waiting, that without receiving his assenting expression or the vibrant reply which, though unaware of how much he gave her, would tell her he had not noticed her sinuous yearning for Ryan, she spoke the thought that broke the spell his silence was casting upon them.

"Oh, Steven," she declared with affecting optimism. "We're going to have such a splendid time."

But even now, in the genteel sight of her influence that was (she permitted herself to imagine) like no other influence upon him except, perhaps, her cool, reviving touch or fragrant-soft elegance, he stood as one alone within the pensive shadings of his stillness. He held his ruddy lips firmly together in some honest covenant or studious alliance that shaped from a smile's vestige and the moment's anchoring stillness a sturdy young man's discomforting apprehension. Though he might from time to time, as an invigorating release from obligations wound like a tight shroud about him, welcome into his own life the perilous unraveling of chance, he saw (apart from the charm of it) her desire to be one with him and with Ryan as well in their plan to soar—reckless and proprietary—above foam-capped waves and clouded, swirling waters as the folly of unjustified risk.

Whether Steven would from that day regard as a similar folly his own forays inside the stark cusp and thrilling clasp of dangerous chance, she (hearing later of all that happened in these hours) did not care to guess, so elliptical and varied were the stories generated by this misadventure of the boating party. Well-schooled as he was, however, in his privileged family's traditions, Steven would have learned, as an essential law of manly honor, that he must do all that could be done to protect a woman from the world's ungoverned harms and sometimes, if need be, from herself. On that July afternoon, then, he may have found no inconsistency between his reluctance to allow her a polite dallying with an imminence of stormy waters and his more serious enthusiasm for launching himself upon the colored flares of perilous time. The race on the sea would be a fiercer way for a promising lawyer to cauterize his wounded senses against a walled-in life of corporate litigation and test as well his most formidable capacities, unused and even buried since his heroic time in the recent war with Germany.

It was, in fact, a formidable test that he and Ryan had devised. For them, a willful race on restless waters made absolute sense, because they brought to their knowledge and love of the sea a joyful athleticism. Theirs was a poised and accurate proficiency that hones its muscular aptitudes on realistic self-appraisal. Not for them the unruly, self-defeating bravado that lacks both wit and mastery. Instead, they claimed an unflinching awareness of the precise radius of their youthful powers and, better still, a respectful apprehension of the monumental sea. That she, with her ethereal perception of things, should want to join them (in what she deemed exotic pastime as easily abandoned as begun) brought him to a sober pause and a nebulous margin of disquiet that Ryan could so casually invite her to the astonishing onrush of risk.

She watched Steven hold himself inside that pause. His darkhaired, rugged demeanor offered still no other sign but coolheaded observation. His was a keen strategy for clarifying an ambiguous moment and arriving at the path on which he might courteously deflect his elegant young lady's compelling idea. So intrigued did he seem by the charm of it and so roused was his reflective glance upon her, that she noticed only gradually the nearly imperceptible reserve that keeps approving words at bay.

It was Ryan, instead, who first recognized his summer friend's lingering introspection as the silent language of reluctance. Impatient by then that they should, nonetheless, hurry on to the afternoon's quickening vibrancies, he spoke the clipped thought that meant to call reliable Steven away from his swift mind's assailing realism.

"You're still game, aren't you?" he asked.

The drift of his words carried a challenge more than a question.

His good-natured ease appearing to return, Steven eyed him more carefully. It was with ungrudging admiration that he studied this tall, lithe arrogance who defined his nature with subtle persuasion, here on a glimmering promontory.

"Why not?"

His words expressed the confidence that he was bringing to the race on the sea awaiting them.

"We'll make a dash for it and, win or lose, have a bit of excitement."

Ryan grinned, a flash of approval tempering the penetrating gaze that said he would hold Steven to his promise.

Hearing this prospect of excitement spoken in the ocean air as though it were an invocation to a playful fury of waters, she smiled her soft exhilaration, still safe and properly modulated.

But the thought he wanted most to convey Steven had not yet declared. So he went forward, finding the words that, after a pause, meant to eclipse this sudden plan that she would join them in their risk.

"The race is between you and me," he told Ryan. "Having Linda with me would be an unfair advantage, because she knows enough about sailing to be a winning partner."

A flicker of Ryan's attention noticed even as it abandoned her wistful demureness. Instead, he accepted face-to-face the full measure of strong-minded Steven, whose sober calm was directing him with apparent effortlessness to a strategy for protecting his fiancée from the day's possible folly. It was then that Ryan sought to disarm his summer friend's waiting protest.

"Oh, the race will be a fair one, no doubt about that," he replied, as if in good faith he were encouraging a fellow athlete, "and we'll be evenly matched."

He saw at once how, with muted surprise, the two of

them, Steven and her, stood watching him now with a tighter stillness. But only after he had turned away from the silver-blue vision of the sea and began walking toward the shadowy edge of the grove did he pause to look back upon them and with crisp affability dispel the moment's mystery.

"We'll be very evenly matched," he said, as though in repetition he might exorcise their new uncertainty and find his way to an enjoyable admission. "After all," he added, his eyes gleaming with what afterwards they told themselves was an amused wiliness, "I'll also have a winning partner."

Though his remark stirred their tentative surprise, they allowed him no other evidence of unease or even the crimson flush of dismay that rises before thoughts of friendship's subtle pledges return to calm and irrigate the senses. So fascinated were they still by his propensity for the unexpected, so proficient was his serpentine maneuvering with chance, that they held unspoken, within the coherent patterns of their courtesy, the brisk question which could draw forth the identity of this winning partner.

Now, without a word to cancel or affirm the verve of their summer bond with him, they (as if compelled by their silent inquiry) followed Ryan along the sloping path that paused discreetly at the edge of the grove. For a moment she imagined that Steven's brother Aaron, with a blunt sufficiency as self-absorbed as it was pragmatic, had decided to test his own athletic prowess in league with a schoolmate who courted with arrogant charm all manner of dangerous possibilities.

But when they returned to the fragrant entrance of the grove, berberis and verbena still glowing with blushed motion beside the fragile whiteness of lavaterra and the wakened shimmer of silver grasses, they at first looked in vain for this mysterious partner. She supposed reasonably that Aaron, all supple brawn and honed-sharp energy, would have skillfully eluded any further contact with his family's elegant summer party and arrived with brusque confidence for the launching of this rugged skirmish with the sea. Only the billowing wind had arrived, though, like a flare of wings lifted by lower winds and pushing upward now against moist, sea-scented air.

This feeling of space actively stirring, this sense that there on a sun-hued promontory the wind had come sweeping through the day's intricate layers and, spinning always its rapid coils, had come to claim them—it was this feeling that stopped their firm gait suddenly and held them in taut surprise back upon their heels while cliffs and clouds and festive summer colors went wheeling by them. The earth itself seemed to revolve with visible motion. She noticed once more the receding diagonals of the grove—a shadow-flecked welling of foliage and trees, an instant's ambiguity of surface and space. She noticed too Ryan's careful scrutiny of that same sequestered place.

Only then did she see her hurrying out of the darkness toward them. Her flowing blonde hair and alabaster radiance granted her the spectral look of a mirage or an apparition. Now, while whorls of slanted light began cautiously to receive her, Linda saw who she was and, seeing, understood, with no need of words to declare or clarify, that her sister, Tracy, was the mysterious partner whom Ryan had chosen.

Though Tracy offered them the courtesy of a charming smile, it was Ryan to whom she gave her excited words.

"Quinn has everything ready," she said. Her voice with Ryan already intimated (or so Linda at once suspected) the hold he had upon her sister.

If a smoldering glance can sometimes convey, as the world's philosophers of feverous love have told us, the heated properties of a sensual embrace, then Ryan had surely enfolded, with the ardor of a burnished look, both body and soul of this willowy girl hurrying toward him as toward a pleasure of the heart. What Linda first saw when her sister emerged from the wind-roused grove was sun-misted light scattering the darkness that hovered about her. Then, but only for a moment, she perceived something altogether astonishing. It was as though her eyes had just then discovered their capacity for divining nature's hidden likenesses—the sudden affinities that shape our new awareness of existing things. For the sun-touched shadow Ryan's vigorous presence cast upon her sister looked so like a looming wave rising to claim her and lifting the ground from under her feet.

"We're ready, too," he casually remarked.

Turning now, he led them away from the grove's fruit-scented threshold. There, flame-orange blooms of potentilla and chestnut-red irises and warm coppery-pink chrysanthemums went on swaying in sensuous ease. He led them as well away from a summer party's evanescent human voices and mellifluous violas and flutes and bassoons and furling surges of the sun-dappled bay. From the comforting southern corner behind them, the heady, resonating wind still wafted sea-and-flower fragrances. Onto the graveled path he brought them, guiding them all the while toward new melodies of wind and waters and to the boat house where old, duty-bound Quinn, the grizzled attendant, waited. It was he whom Ryan had privately directed (she surmised, on hearing Tracy's exhilarated words) to prepare two boats for launching.

Quinn's gruff heartiness and cynical enjoyment of the unexpected would, she knew from first-hand experience, quicken his willingness to carry out Ryan's directive.

Not without his own appreciation of Ryan's unorthodox devices for subverting the humdrum and familiar, Steven (she sensed) found himself resenting nonetheless, just a little, the younger man's proprietary maneuvering of their day. Perhaps he really meant that afternoon to thwart this wild youth's plan to parry with the restless sea. With his own brisk confidence, he hurried along the glimmering path, a haze like blue flax already rising to encoil them. Placing his large, athletic hand on his new friend's shoulder, Steven persuaded him to pause.

"You're very sure of us," he said, his words held firm inside a tighter huskiness.

No sooner had he spoken, than they, he and Ryan, studied each other with a keen steadiness. A soldierly stillness allowed them time to gather the sum of each other's meaning. Now, as if to declare the language by which they could in affable fraternity go forward, Ryan chose the agreeable words that would keep them on their course.

"I'm sure of all my friends," he said, a flicker of a smile tracing his matter-of-factness.

Was that the moment when she might have, by speaking honest words, saved them all from the unhappy excitement that followed? Was it then that she might have saved all of them by choosing to utter an uncomplicated language that resisted Ryan's undermining their safe priorities?

(For weeks afterwards Linda wondered, while remembering the apparent playfulness of that festive afternoon, which only in retrospect seemed colored falsely, like a tinted sky concealing immensities of storm.)

But she did not speak the precise words which might have held all of them to their proper course. Without anything but the compass of affection to guide us into new, exuberant fellowship, how does the heart measure accurately the motives of another human being? She had accepted Ryan, as she had accepted Steven. With their careful breeding and aristocratic textures, they were in different ways extraordinary. Each of them was a dynamic presence, inviting her to broaden, and perhaps deepen, the enigmatic circumference of herself—the always-changing, mysterious perimeters of her never-completely-charted nature. No, she did not speak the proper words that might have saved all of them. She had no art to decipher the unknown or to guess that a playful boat race on the sea and its abrasive aftermath would be sufficient occasion for disarranging their lives and making grievous recollection a constant, visible scene.

Steven, though, had meant to speak out. With level-headed inquiry, he approached this enterprising youth whom he had come to regard as a secret blood brother or foster spirit reflecting his own life-quickening capacities.

But he yielded the moment, nevertheless, to whatever plan that chance or fate or willful Ryan or she herself cared to impose upon a restless summer day.

Some might say that it was she, not arbitrary fate or random chance or wily Ryan, who now influenced the yet-alterable pattern their casual day without much notice was weaving. It was she who arrived at the secluded spot where Steven and Ryan were conferring. There in the blue haze of the sun-tinged graveled path, she delicately touched her fiancé's rugged arm. Quite naturally he looked her way and, noticing her elated eyes, comprehended without a word or any gesture other than the graceful touch of her fingers the currents of her quiet desire.

If she influenced the pendulous swing of that moment, it was perhaps the cool touch of her fingers upon Steven's heated skin and the elated glow of her eyes that moved him to speak the very words his canny judgment had meant to withhold from the festive afternoon which all of a sudden, an hour or so later, would pitch and slope away from them.

"You've a mind for sailing," he said, with a clipped directness that made his simple language sound vigorous and original.

She in turn smiled a discreet assent, her words held still in silence. Only a poised, nearly imperceptible nod affirmed her reply.

"Then we'll sail," he jauntily beamed, "though the four of us will, I think, be racing mainly the weather."

Her satisfied heart allowed her to answer this time with unrestrained clarity.

"We'll have a marvelous time."

Perhaps it was the prospect of an afternoon's swift sport on the sea which satisfied her, or Steven's enthusiasm for her quiet desire, which he chose to interpret not as a passing whim, but an ardent need. Just as possibly it was the stir of pleasure she felt in deflecting her disarranged expectation that she alone would be the woman soaring recklessly with Ryan through the temporary afternoon.

Or, more likely, it was her clear-sighted though uneasy awareness of how the day's indirections had delivered her from herself. A sometime familiar stranger to herself, she had allowed this wild youth, this subtle cruelty called Ryan Turner, to take hold of her mind and spirit for an hour or two and then, as sated with her as if he had claimed her physically as well, to turn indifferently away.

Whether it was any one of these things which saved or satisfied her or only some of them or none at all, she did not know. While from time to time silently recounting that day, she never fully clarified herself to herself, intuiting perhaps that none of us can parcel out our motives by geometric rules or split our desires like a territory coiling into round or perpendicular.

As if her words were a promise that the rising trees and whirl of winds and wheels over wheels of summer-bay waters would excite the slanting afternoon just enough to exhilarate their senses and give a boat race on a tilting sea a surge of safer peril, they hurried down to the waiting dock and gleaming yawls and gnarled curmudgeon Quinn.

His mumbled inflections were both warning and solicitude which he directed toward all of them and toward Steven most of all, for Quinn had served the Bradfords for thirty years and more.

"There's a stronger wind behind this one, Mr. Bradford."

"A strong wind's what we have in mind, Quinn," Steven asserted with a boldness that enjoys itself. "Today we're going to ride her."

So confident did Steven seem, so caught up was he by this billowing energy of the unexpected, that self-willed Ryan, for the last minute or so having consented to the convolutions of his own observing stillness, called out to them with typical ease, as though his spoken thought were by itself a vigor that would prevail over the swerving chances of that hour.

"Now we'll have a real adventure," he said.

No sooner had he done so than they heard, as an ancillary influence or perhaps an independent power, Tracy's impassioned elation. Her words, as Steven and she remembered them afterward, were yearning and still innocent, a romantic girl's heartfelt and wistful hope.

"We'll have days and days of adventure," she said. "We'll have whole years of happiness."

While she spoke, descending with them the path to the jetty and the waiting boats, she whirled about as in a dance. She was a graceful flowing of summer garments and golden hair.

As she perceived her, Tracy appeared to be confirming, rather than claiming as new, the full-bodied colors of her nature. In her eyes, the joyous rush of imagery which on this day her sister represented was but one of a hundred plausible variations of the person that she already was. It might have been, as well, a suppressed or evolving version of herself she had not sufficiently tested.

She had in these few weeks of her family's visit with the Bradfords, here within this luminous seascape that so admirably quickened the senses, impressed her as someone ancillary or incidental to the life-loving and effectual girl that she had been before their mother died. It was as if, by collaborating with their father's grief, she was learning to live with stinted powers.

Once, while she and Steven sauntered barefoot by the sea, along early morning's gleaming white sand that waited to be touched by the sinuous ripples of sun-flecked waters, they saw Tracy coming toward them from out of a mist-shrouded distance. Her willowy grace stood not alone, but in lingering consonance with her father, as if reluctant to travel away from his tightly-wrought sorrow. Later, on an afternoon when they were returning from their own sauntering along the path that glided beside the shimmering meadow behind the west wing of the house, they watched her from afar. Alone then, she was lovely in a white-flowing cotton dress and an azure parasol. Strolling along the deserted beach, she was looking out over the wide expanse of a restless sea, compelled by a vision they had not yet apprehended.

It was only when she moved too quickly toward the breaking waves that for an instant they believed she was going to drown herself. Calling her name in apprehensive voices that fell beneath the crash of the breakers and inside the restless winds, they ran across the space which separated her from them. But when they reached her willowy form, they received an altogether different impression. She had (they told themselves) stepped back from the sea and now wore a look of surprise that the breaking waves had wet her dress. Caught as she was within her weary unhappiness, she had not realized that she was walking so dangerously close to the sea.

When she turned to them, aware now that they had hurried there to watch her with curious eyes, she gently took their hands into hers. She seemed grateful that they stood so protectively beside her.

"The sea is restless today," she said. "That's when I love it most of all. It tells me that my restlessness may be a natural thing, too."

She sensed the tension in her sister. Her careful voice could not conceal the fact that she had been crying.

Steven noticed, too. With easy courtesy, he offered her words meant to call her away from her sorrow.

"Let's be restless together," he said. "I'm sure that you, Linda, and I can find an adventure or two during these next weeks."

Almost imperceptibly, she held his hand more firmly. Her tearful eyes brightened momentarily. But her lips could not compose the affectionate smile she had often given him so easily.

Influenced by Steven's sympathetic manner, she began coaxing Tracy away from her brooding.

"Mother wouldn't want you to grieve like this," she told her. "She would want you to make the best of things."

Tracy paused, as if she were weighing the realism of the thought.

"How can I, when Father is so unhappy?"

"Your father will put this hard time behind him," Steven said. "You must do the same."

She paused again. Then, with reluctant words which were soft at first and tremulous, she addressed the both of them through new tears.

"I wish I could be like Father," she lamented. "I wish I could love Mother as he does, as though she were alive and with us."

Before this sight of her grieving sister, she took pause. Older than Tracy by five years and away at private schools and, afterward at Bryn Mawr, she had been, for the most part, unavailable as the helpful counselor and nurturing friend she would surely have chosen to be, had there not been so wide a disparity between their ages and had their daily activities put them more in the way of each other. Not even when she returned home to help care for her dying mother did she find herself in her sister's presence, for Tracy herself was then away at school. In those rare times when they *were* in each other's company, she tried to be a friend to her. But she had sensed that Tracy, always polite and often lighthearted, preferred to keep her at a distance. She associated her, perhaps, with the grown-ups whom she regarded as authority figures rather than as friends.

From time to time she had been very pleased to notice her sister conversing affably with others on the sun-glanced terrace of their Newport home—their father perhaps or one of the Norwegian or Chinese girls who attended her school and, as a guest in their seaside residence for a month or so, was sharing with the family summer's lighthearted activities. But on one occasion, when she had entered the library without expecting to find anyone there, she met the somber pensiveness of her sister, coiled as she was within its traces. On a different afternoon she had observed her too-still quietude in the shadowy light of the drawing room window from which she was wistfully peering. Only on those days had she noticed what, later, Steven would tell her he also had perceived. A tincture of sadness was enshrouding Tracy's bright surfaces. There was in her a nearly imperceptible suggestion of private sorrow and a tint of weariness, sequestered and momentary.

Steven remembered that in previous years Tracy had been life-loving and exuberant. In those days all of the Maguires, including their mother, had from their own neighboring home summered with the Bradfords as a family whole and integral. Always, Tracy inspirited a scene with her quick-witted and affable nature.

To observe her in these recent weeks of his knowing her once more, however, was to receive her not as herself or as a total stranger even, but as someone altogether unexpected. She was somebody different, if not completely separate—a reflection of a vital girl he felt he had known and accurately remembered. The imagery of herself in full bloom now told his apprehension none the less who she used to be and taught his eyes to receive her as a distinctive counterpart to the happy girl he remembered seeing from time to time with her parents before the war. To his present glance, the anguish that she held within herself was an authentic part of her essence. This additional layer of her existence had only in these summer weeks disclosed itself to his sudden capacity for seeing within the imagery that was herself exactly as he had anticipated someone revised for his comprehension.

Yet never—not even in these hard months after their mother's death—had Tracy of her own volition revealed to her by outward sign or shared confidence any unhappiness or dismay, except perhaps for the tears a young girl sometimes sheds because of a day's fleet disappointment. For that reason, she—being a discreet older sister—resolved never to intrude upon so intricate a process as her sister's individuality. But always she maintained toward her a warm and earnest demeanor, as spontaneous as it was decorous. Had her sister ever called out to her for encouragement or assistance or rescue of any kind, she would have gladly and effectually answered. But Tracy had never called out to her. It was only now, in the roused uneasiness of a wind-swept afternoon, that she had quite by chance apprehended the truth of her sister's deep-rooted sorrow. Only now, without intending to do so, did her sister call to her and call as clearly to Steven.

"I want to be happy again," she said as they walked

with her back to the house. "I want to feel free of all care, because it is summer and because I am young."

"We'll help you find your way back to yourself," Steven told her. "We'll show you how to be happy again."

His husky friendliness ignited brotherly capacities, and the affection in his glance brought the hint of a smile to her lips.

"For the rest of this summer," she assured her sister, "you are going to enjoy everything."

In the weeks that followed, she and Steven orchestrated days and days of happiness for her. Always, they drew to her an enthusiastic company of athletic youths and poised young ladies who had become her loyal friends through the years. At times, other parents joined her and Steven as chaperones who kept themselves at a respectful distance that allowed Tracy and her friends a proper latitude for navigating their individuality.

As a life-loving group, they first kayaked along the Sakonnet River in nearby Tiverton. There, after paddling to Blue Bell Cove just west of the river's basin, they explored the picturesque islands and beaches. In Sakonnet Point a few days later, they journeyed on their bicycles through a rambling scenic trail. It was a lift to their spirits, upon reaching the village of Little Compton, to ride past the expansive wetlands and pastures.

During the following week, as exuberant as ever, the

group visited a farm on Aquidneck Island which recalled an eighteenth-century Swiss Village. As though they had entered a long-ago past, they traversed its thirty-two acres in 1840 Seabrook Carriages that were pulled by American Cream draft horses. All around them they saw green, undulating pastures, rugged and ample trees, and sun-glistening ponds. Behind the main house, which was constructed of rough-cut rock that had been blasted out of the surrounding ledge, rhododendron bushes soared to generous heights. They saw as well, in pastures some distance from the home field, Randall Lineback cattle, Belted Galway cows, Florida cracker horses, Tennessee Myotonic goats, and Gulf Coast sheep. Irregular stone bollards kept horses and carriages on the pebble roadway that went winding through the farm. Occasionally, an exotic bird sauntered by a pond or chose a guard-rail as its resting place.

From her perch in a carriage with Steven and with the engaging Morrisons, whose son and daughter were among the most gregarious in the group, she could see Tracy and her peers in a carriage that was hurrying just ahead of their own. Neal and Carolyn Morrison were there with her, and so was Ryan Turner. In that moment it cheered her to see Tracy looking buoyant and receptive as she shared lighthearted anecdotes with her friends.

Most memorable of all their excursions, so Tracy told

her and Steven afterward, was their climb to Ferry Cliff in Bristol County. On that day their group included only six persons. Besides Steven, Tracy and her, there were Ryan Turner and the young Morrisons—Neal and Carolyn. During these hours, Ryan appeared to give far more attention to the Morrison girl than to Tracy. It was Neal Morrison who actively courted her sister's interest. To him she responded with an easy blitheness.

But only intermittently had she noticed her sister and the others.

Instead, she gave herself almost completely to the new experience of climbing to the highest ridge which peered over Bristol Harbor. There, just beyond the nest of a white-eared hummingbird and beyond windswept tufts of grass, she saw and heard—as for the first time because so near her and actual—the quickened wingbeat of a herring gull. With Steven on that same ridge, she also observed the sun resting on a bank of clouds where its light shone brighter and more neutral. A ghostly mist disturbed the hill below them and touched as well the sailboats and ships that were leaving or returning to the harbor. In that moment she perceived in a different way the curving surfaces of the sea.

"You've brought me to life again," Tracy told Steven and her one morning a few days afterward. They had just enjoyed a brisk swim in the Bradfords' cantilevered pool that flowed into the waters of the Atlantic. "I have never been so happy."

"The summer will be with us for many weeks," she told her. "Steven and I are planning other special days for you and your friends."

"We promised you a good time," Steven said, "and we intend to keep our word."

Her sister was delighted at the prospect of being with them and with her friends.

"I had almost forgotten all the wonderful and familiar things that can make me happy."

Hearing her elated words, she and Steven were very pleased. They had rescued her from all her sorrow. They had shown her how to call back the self she had lost after their mother's death.

Now, four weeks later, they were heartened once more to find that she was joining them in the day's unexpected flare of surprise. Her bright anticipation brought them a new pleasure. Surely, this boat race over restless waters would satisfy her need to be in the world, new and self-reliant and evolving.

2

So they sailed into the unfurling wind, receiving it still as a gift for their senses. It was both echoing melody and wafting sea-fragrance. It was elusive caress and cloud-driving impetus. Already the sky was discarding its cerulean textures and revealing with incautious spontaneity bruised grays and violets and crimsons. But the dazzle and warm lilt of that late afternoon shimmered yet across their youthful spirits. Still it dispensed the crispness of its favor and betrayed none of its promise for their venture-laden expectations.

Linda remembered that first hour on the bay as a series of indirections and a discovery of unexpected inclines and sinuous turnings. It seemed in the sheer lift and pulse of her enthusiasm as though they, in their sailboats leaving the shore, were disengaging themselves from essential roots and anchors and foundations. That fleet portion of the world unfurling before her heart-quickened senses was all disengagement and even dislocation. It was a swift disjoining of earth's safer boundaries not only from the intricate transitions of the bay, but from the ballast and equilibrium of the familiar, as well.

There, beyond the brine-green wake of waters whose roiling track glistened on the brisk sea's disarrangement— right there, while before the lilt and glow of her backward glance the shoreline in rapid motion eluded with an agile geometry the summer waves' wily incursions— just there, at the sun-glanced line where the furrowing sea arced toward the shore, the land leaped, tensile and accurate and then swerved and spun and scrolled, scattering whole houses and trees and summer people. Or so it seemed to her excited senses.

So it seemed as with comfortable acumen she eased the yawl's white-flashing jibsheets to test the wind's new, supple currents and afterwards, as her limber Steven with synchronous powers taught the mainsail to scan both risk and necessity. So to her it all so marvelously seemed in the thrill and push of her flourishing awareness that this wayward afternoon could find its meaning in their unexpected departure from the land and in their undeclared surrender of all the places that knew them. It found its meaning as well in their leave-taking of the selves they had so often compassed and, paradoxically, in their willful arrival before the convoluted mysteries of the sea and before their own mysteries and convolutions.

Now, while turning toward wind-raveling waters and sun-clasped clouds and the floating haze of chrome green hills across the bay, she noticed—as though he were a prowess as intricate as the sea—magnificent Ryan Turner. He was hiking out over the gunwales of his craft, his ruggedness tethered by canvas straps to his yawl's brisk velocity. Vivid and actual, he was in her approving eyes like the sun-gold youth from nautical stories taming a wily dolphin or like some unknown sea-god with a mind for balancing a sailboat as well as ocean winds and waters. And there beside Ryan while hiking with him to windward was exhilarated Tracy. Leaning assured and proprietary into hastening space just beyond their heeling vessel, she appeared at that very instant to be rising from foam-covered waves glancing off their boat's zinc-white hull.

Impossible it was to keep but a moment, in the surging awareness of her senses, this imagery of Tracy and Ryan as confident allies of the day's rapid processes. So smoothly did they bring their craft to a confluent swiftness and balance that the burnished imagery that was themselves navigating their vessel hastened into the sun-flecked recessions of space before her, where the blue-opal distance kept spiraling backward. So much brighter than day were they to her eyes on that occasion that even the sea appeared to part its vigorous waters. It was as if for them alone together, for daring Ryan and vital Tracy, there grew voluminous and tactile a faster corridor hurrying them away from the lift and flare of her fleeting glance toward a territory of bold cutters and catboats, a half-dozen or more, glimmering above the churning push of darker waters.

But farther than that even, though before the pulsing skyline sloped and spun within a haze of hills—just before— there, on wind-flung waves and teeming mist, a solitary yawl rippled like flickering light, gold-orange and amber and viridian silver. Then, because new radiance above the yawl directed her attention, she saw a cadre of glaucous-winged gulls pursuing hidden curvatures of sunlight and air and rose-tinted cloud. Only minutes after that, in the flurrying distance, she glimpsed inlet and bay, greenscape and grove, and the silver-blue sheen of a promontory. Yet sometimes she understood—in an instant—glint of meadow and gleam of farm-field and congregant trees stirring like celestial bodies. Suddenly, even then in that race across the bay, she knew again as palpable and actual the hard-bodied whiteness of a waiting lighthouse. And always, while with her rugged Steven she became on rapid waters a collateral emphasis, she felt summer-warm winds spilling around them as from a sail of the quick, mysterious earth.

But the wind, aromatic still with sweet-bitter scent of ruckled waters and land-spawned flower fragrances, occasionally held back its sea-driving favor. At the very moment that Ryan and Tracy hurried past them, beyond the swift recoil of waking waters, the wind with blunt surprise struck their sails, hers and her athletic Steven's, on the lee side. It enclosed them within its torpid shadow (what mariners call the blanket zone) and annulled at once their boat's nimble powers. Held aloft, with tension poised, their sails waited.

No sooner had Ryan, all the while racing with furious ease, deflected the wind's force away from Steven's sail, than with his own formidable seamanship inspiriting him Steven trimmed his boat's main sheet close-hauled. Only afterwards, when the forward edge of his sail began to ripple, did he find a proper path for making his way out of the imprisoning blanket zone into a soaring vigor that was freedom once more and new-claimed velocity. Then his craft knew boundlessness horizontal and leaping and knew as well curving verticality, so often leaning and sometimes precarious.

So in this swifter flash of late afternoon did she and Steven approach again the fluency that was Ryan and Tracy sailing across the hastening span of the sea. But never could they surpass them or gain a leeward power to send a stalling backwind upon them. Yet how vigorously and with supple acumen did Steven pilot their vessel's bold maneuverings. She herself activated the adventure with him. She with him kept riding the crest of hurling chance—and they together a brave and ardent reciprocity. Rarely had exhilaration for them together been as supreme as in that billowing hour of risk. Awareness became a crisper form of breathing as when they two, navigating a momentous soaring of the senses, a surging of will and pulse and aptitude, noticed—as a mirror of their own becoming—Ryan and Tracy riding across space and time so fearlessly. For the wind-whipped bucking world, its sea and land and altitude as well, was theirs to test and tame and possess, at least for a flourishing sun-gold season.

Once again this brave imagery of Ryan and Tracy rising over the crest of luminous waters glanced back at their apprehension, hers and Steven's, and hurried onward, as if the radiance in which they rode belonged to them alone and only they were their parallel. Yet even together Ryan Turner and Tracy Maguire were each of them a self distinct and italic. Their individuality remained buoyant and whole all the while they were so joyously there together. Only obliquely did they surrender the identity that separately was each of them, intrinsic.

It was the clarity of this recognition that heartened her. For it validated her earlier intuition that she and Steven, married, would be a fusion of so many evolving identities. They would be infinite-seeming versions and revisions of their differences and of their mutuality. How wonderful, she'd thought, to be alive and young and original, even as one's self enfolded another—even as one's soul and spirit and always-quickened mind embraced the pulse and throb of existence as a discovery absolutely new—experience inwoven and singular.

Now it was that she declared, because the wily day had shown her the danger that was in herself, the sheer thrill of ascending the curve and slope of that afternoon with catapulting chance beside her.

"There's so much adventure here, and we are a part of it," she told Steven as he stood by the tiller, looking toward the blue-green margins of the horizon. Hearing her words, he turned to her reflectively. Then with an assured muscularity he reached out to caress her shoulder, as if by a lover's touch he could enter whatever new mystery was welling within her.

He laughed a deep-hearted laugh, easing his way into her elation, and then spoke the thought that was as a fuse to her excitement.

"*We* are the adventure."

So it seemed to their excited senses. So, even and especially in the last rapturous moments of their race on the bay, it all so wonderfully seemed while the wily day, glimmering now within intricacies of mist, cast a spectral glow upon them and upon everything they could see. The whole of reality, or at least the portion of the world which they together were beholding, seemed to disappear gradually. Perhaps (she mused) the oblique surrender of identity was a fundamental law not only of adventure, but of everything else that was coherent and plausible and apparently real.

Still they apprehended the light and colors of exhilaration. Still they could see in the rapid distance before them the flare of yawls and catboats and cutters. From time to time they discovered, fearless and exuberant, Ryan and Tracy riding on the crest of new venturing. Sun-fused clouds went on waiting and the ample sky leaned, languorous and approving, upon playful, iridescent waters. All the while, as the greenery of the land leaped and the ambivalent shoreline swerved, she with her accomplished Steven reveled at the very rim of that day's taut harmonies.

Then the afternoon turned to other purposes. The air glowed with lightning-flame. Its gash of orange-yellow and eerie glaze of umber and green gave notice of impending wildness. Roused suddenly, winds pushed away whole alliances of clouds, gone dark-bruised gray and indigo. The sky billowed, disarranged as the bay rose and cascaded. Space—welling backward—disappeared within curves of haze and on the roiling timbres of thunder and, just as suddenly, returned to align itself with familiar outlines of day. New light erupted from a pearl-gray vortex of clouds, saturating hills and sky and sea and covering as well sailboats that leaned more than rode upon pulsing waters. That was the storm's enigmatic harbinger for the next half-hour or more, while late afternoon, understanding perhaps the strategies of storm, fulfilled ordinary obligations and waited.

How long the storm would wait, ambivalently reconciled with its stinted powers, neither she nor Steven paused to guess. For there had been, valued and remembered, other days in their experience of the sea when wind and wave and velocity, each of them reconnoitering and inflective, had held back their assailing powers temporarily. Only then did shafts of sunlight and rich vitalities of color gradually return to reconstruct what had so swiftly been dislocated or dispelled or lost even: the more affable sensations of summer's reality vibrant over sail-worthy waters. How, after all, when the storm had already shown its belligerent features, could pausing avail them or any other boatman riding those uncertain waters? No, they did not pause to guess at the sea's imminent heft and swell and turbulent ascensions. Instead, with a mariner's gift for interpreting the weather's equivocal language and with her in mind first of all, Steven resolved that he must pilot his craft away from the storm's waiting powers.

"We'll go back," he calmly told her.

A skillful sailor herself needing no other explanation, she smiled in quick-witted agreement. (They, both of them, were a bright splendor in sun-gold oilskins and with the energy of knowledgeable motion.)

So, easing the tiller slowly and rounding up into a favorable wind, he brought his craft skillfully about. After trimming flat and relying now on his storm sail alone, he began the journey homeward.

Still the storm withheld for a time its wilder capacities while, proficient and exhilarated yet, they sailed by way of Dyer Island, to the Bradfords' estate near Brenton Point. It was wonderful then, and more so than at the start of their race, to see in the opaque-blue furling of distance the floating pastel sky. They could see as well, soaring on gleaming curve and flash, the vigorous whiteness of herring gulls and near the crest of viridian clouds—or seeming so— the gray-blue immensity of swaying larches. More palpable than those because nearer and emphatic, hills and cliffs and farm field flared upon their seeing. Boats iridescent and angular hastened toward the harboring comforts of land. By guile or skill or favorable chance their pilots had outraced the pulsing afternoon's sterner insurrections.

As for that other race, Steven's formidable contest with Ryan, what the two of them had agreed would be a realistic calculation of their seamanship and of the boats whose speed they'd be commanding—as for that race, Ryan had claimed a solid victory. For that reason, she and Steven anticipated that this shrewd interpreter of the sky's signs and portents and of a fleet rival's surprised eclipse would regard the race as his and with canny foresight navigate his vessel homeward. There he would revel amiably and not with the preening self-regard that uses victory to deny the skills of an enterprising comrade. Instead, Ryan would, they believed, recognize an opponent's merit. More than that, he would salute the bond between athletic peers which had drawn into their fraternity two proficient young ladies who brought to a nautical adventure their own extemporaneous daring.

While they hastened across the subtle billow of waters that seemed as sensitive to the flicker of a pushing wind as to the aureate-blueness of an ambiguous sky, Steven would, from time to time, look back at the flash of catboats and cutters not far behind him. He expected to find Ryan and Tracy rising assured and splendid with their sailboat, there in the loom and sweep of onrushing nearness—right there, on the curve and slope and crescent slant of the sea. But only the wind rose then, its gathered powers held tense and indeterminate within a throbbing nature.

Later, a half-hour or so, while their sailboat skimmed across the wheeling bay, they at the rudder discovered new the zinc-white hang of wind-bleached cliffs glaring like the sea-tossed bones of a devoured world. Right after that with startled awareness they looked back at the rugged sky and ragged clouds and uneasy surge of waters thrown into the pivoting hurl of receding distance. Then, reassured and believing, they saw splendid Ryan and exhilarant Tracy hurrying windward toward them while scaling sea-whelmed altitudes of risk—all its gravity and mass and supple fervencies.

How comforting in that moment to witness out of their hope and expectation the elated presence of Ryan and Tracy riding on the cantering sea. But all too soon gusts of prismatic light and rippled outlines and surfaces subverted as mirage or illusion what they were seeing. Before their eyes Ryan and Tracy disappeared. Not without a tinge of wistful humor, she and Steven understood with pensive dismay that they had been seeing what was not there. They had been devising rather than finding the solacing imagery which in too-excited apprehension they beheld.

As they arrived home and the wind, bestirred, was pushing them into the shadow-flecked dock, they lowered their storm sail and with quicksilver motion rolled and lashed it to the boom, around which they had looped the mainsheet so that with one pull on the end it could, as if gliding, unravel. Adept and precise, Steven now guided the tiller in and turned broadside to the dock just before reaching it. Then old, grizzled Quinn hobbled along the pier to meet the heave of Steven's mooring line and, afterwards, struggle onto the boat to help them cover the boom with tarpaulin. They tied it snugly over the furled sail and at the sides below the gunwales, with both ends left open to keep air moving through. They meant to store the vessel in the boathouse, away from the heft and hurl of the summer storm.

Once more they looked back to the dark, rougher waters that were roiled again and voyaging alone. By this time whole squadrons of catboats and cutters and yawls had hurried back to other jetties and piers and private docks near or within Brenton Point. Some of them had hurried forward to charted destinations or unexpected harbors away from home—and beyond the horizon of violet-grays and reds and orange-yellows that to their searching eyes flickered like temporary flame or a vaguely perceptible beacon. As they looked back, they paused on the rim of uneasy apprehension to confirm what their eyes and reason and intuition had already taught them. Ryan and Tracy would not in that hour be returning. Nor would they return in any of the other hours which with jagged and weighty powers were still to influence that wayward afternoon.

Massive burnt-umber clouds, cumulous and sky-welling and with the wind proprietary over the sea, were heralding further inroads of storm. Why Ryan had chosen to outrace this eddying risk, she and Steven could not—except prodded as they were by the doubtful accuracy of surmise—begin to fathom. Perhaps, Ryan had consented so intensively to the race on the sea, that he had no need to justify safe hesitation or the prudent retreat that promises security even while subverting the adventurous purposes inspiriting a young man's bold nature.

Or possibly the very turbulence of the impending storm had quickened his determination to race not against Steven, but against wind and wave and sky. Or a calculated desire to wage battle with chance and accident had eclipsed his otherwise shrewd appraisal of things—his realistic awareness of options and probabilities. Or, just as likely, he expected the storm to be as brief as it was wild and, thus, unable to prevent his returning with Tracy in a few hours.

Whatever the truth of things that would in time echo clearly, they had no misgivings about Ryan's ability to deliver Tracy and himself to the sanctuary of a convenient shore or distant island. He was an accomplished adventurer on the sea. His tested skill and hardened agility were a far more convincing surety than too-cautious aptitude or dutiful mediocrity.

No, she—like Steven—had not one misgiving about Ryan's confident proficiencies or about the resourceful equipoise which he had always maintained between his aggressive sailing and the sea's arbitrary fluctuations.

Rather, it was the thought of Tracy that gave her pause. Her sister's venturousness was a complicated imagery that perplexed even while it appealed to her solicitude for her. That Tracy's casual repudiation of safe convention—this rebellious hour soaring alone with Ryan across a storm-rankled bay—could do her much harm, she was uneasily aware. Though, in league with Ryan, she might well elude the sea's fiercer convolutions, her sister could, because of carefree behavior perceived as reckless and sensual, compromise her good name.

That they, each of them singular and attentive and witnessing the world as if new in their seeing, were expected to represent established traditions and rigorous standards and the subtle codes which were the language of their rank and prerogative, Linda's matter-of-fact understanding of their social group's ruling constraints and judgments wisely acknowledged. In that summer of 1920, the men and women who were the leaders of the privileged society to which they belonged observed the four of them and appraised, as though they might prove valued possessions, the resilience and integrity of their characters. They noted subtleties of gesture and spirited assurance and searched out all the hidden correspondences between intimating outlines and colorful surfaces and that startling emphasis individuality. All the while they imposed upon the estimated imagery that was apparently themselves, four young beings evolving, permissible definitions that carried with them the vested interpretations of an entire class.

So she understood, pensive in her uneasiness about Tracy and Ryan riding together over ominous waters. But only for a moment would she allow these thoughts to give her pause.

Perhaps it was at this time that she felt the full weight of her unease, with its complicated structures of quiet disdain for society's narrowness and troubling surprise at Ryan's casual regard of Tracy's safety and of her reputation. She had turned with Steven away from the dock and had noticed in the lift and flare of her hurrying glance whole shafts of raveling sunlight pierce a brooding mass of ocher and gray-blue clouds. A moment after that, Quinn called out to Steven the question that prodded the pulse of his discomfort. With three young workmen, the aged mariner was preparing to carry the yawl from shoreline waters to the boathouse nearby. It was exactly then that she felt the full weight of her unease.

(So she explained to Olivia, Steven's mother, hours later, recounting to her that wayward day while the Coast Guard kept searching for Tracy and Ryan.)

What she so clearly recollected were the raspy timbres of Quinn's gravel-rough voice and the grizzled features of that hard, wily man meeting directly Steven's own inquiring frown. His young, furrowed brow had been a way to evoke once more from a tough old sailor the simple words that had been overtaken by the rippling wind's taut fluctuations.

"Will Mr. Turner and the young lady be coming back today?"

It was Steven's turn now, upon hearing the echo of Quinn's question, to repeat himself by once more looking back at the sinuous disarrangement of indigo waters, which were sun-flashing still, yet restless. To her eyes, they were almost aggressive.

"I don't know" was all he cared to answer.

Then, with well-honed watchfulness and while pausing with her on the path to his parents' summer home, he scanned once again the storm-imminent waters. Their ambiance of gold and purple still rode over umber traces while he searched for other signs of Ryan and Tracy sailing homeward across the roused velocities of that nearly completed afternoon. But only the wind hurried forward, a welling of currents like wilder symmetries. Hurrying, too, were the leaning verticalities of hills and trees on the southwest rim of the bay. Nearer than that and more emphatic, a sudden trio of sloops, gray-white and wave-tossed, headed for other harbors. Still the tang and fumes and fish-scent of the sea teased the senses. Suddenly a roiling of sun-rippled clouds and lightning ignited raw tension upon the billowing land.

Turning now from this flare of chance and ominous energy, this flash and surge and italic notice of the day's hazardous aptitudes, she and Steven met the silver-stone path that brought them to the north wing of the house. Unobtrusively they found their way inside a private entrance and the seclusion of his father's study. Once there, amidst the solace of pastel walls, they were all the while conscious of newer clarities and crispness and the cool harmonies of opaque blue. They knew again the plush of a Beauvais carpet, ample chairs and desk of cherry wood, and gilt-edged bookshelves with special editions. On the periphery of their seeing, outdoors with the storm-glimmering afternoon and brushing against the beveled window they sequestered, swaying profusions of golden leaves and red-winged fruit belonged to an aureum maple.

In the heightened awareness of all these sensuous things, she stood before an illuminating portrait of Steven's parents. As if she had come to this room for that very purpose, she studied their quiet strength and the quiet felicities of their union. Then, she turned to Steven, who was already speaking to someone from his father's personal house-phone. He was telling Chapman, the indispensable overseer of their large and demanding Newport home, that it was necessary for the senior Mr. Bradford and Mr. Maguire to confer with him in the study.

3

"You've done all that can be done," Steven's father asserted, without suggesting that his son's swiftness in alerting the Coast Guard about Ryan and Tracy's being caught somewhere over storm-lashed waters would necessarily resolve their peril or any of the other unexpected dispositions of the last hour or two.

Nor would her father allow himself even the hint of a frown, to his disciplined mind a prosaic sign of dismay, that Steven had, by consenting to a reckless venturing with the sea, too casually relaxed his guardian care of others and of himself. She sensed that he recognized none the less the mute anxiety that Steven was holding at bay because of his self-command and his keen-eyed intelligence.

Without attracting to themselves any gratuitous

inquiry, the two men had drawn away from the festive summering ongoing still, though no longer in the surge and sway of wind-roused greenery or on the splendid flower-redolent terrace. The guests, she learned, had hurried from the storm into spacious rooms that married Tudor stateliness to the Bradfords' witty evocation of a pastoralism offering the simplicity of its natural powers to an artful elegance. This sumptuous July happiness, this tincture of illusion belonging to their privileged class, seemed therefore never completely separated from the earthbound gravity of the real. In due time Daniel Bradford and her father had withdrawn from that magnificent array of rooms where the exuberant voices and self-reflexive conversations of the guests accepted the more mellifluous intonations of piano and flute and viola. They accepted as well from outside a surround of French doors the disharmonies of roused winds and roiling thunder.

In curious apprehension they had arrived to notice, there inside the hushed ambiance of Daniel's study, the austerities of Steven's and her responses. Steven's clipped speech and stoic demeanor and tautened physicality would—she was certain—suggest at once that something was wrong.

(She was aware that these senior men knew Steven well—Daniel because he was his father and her own father because he was Steven's godparent. With quiet appreciation, they were acquainted with many of his virtues. They regarded him as an admirable war hero. Right after law school, Steven had fought with hardened fury at Cambrai and Messines and afterwards at St. Mihiel. At the last, he'd fought in the Meuse-Argonne offensive, where the enemy's bullet pierced his body at a point only an inch or so from his heart. Until that moment, he had heard all around him the rapid, incessant guns and fired alongside his platoon his own stuttering rifle's accurate bullets. Bitter experience it was to see his closest comrades die like cattle, sometimes in the cool of a sunlit morning when their muscular bodies, meeting the enemy's volleys, lifted and broke apart.

Time and circumstance had tested Steven and found him to be strong-willed and brave. During these few years succeeding the war, he had found his way back to a promising life. Only recently, scrupulous directors had in pleased unanimity invited him to a junior partnership with the international association of lawyers in which the Bradfords—Daniel and his brother—and the Tomlinsons—his wife's father and uncle—shared with British and French colleagues the primary influences.)

When these older men had in heightened awareness arrived at Daniel's study, they noticed not only the stoic demeanor of her reliable Steven. They noticed as well within her face an unanticipated stillness and a careful reserve.

Arriving there to meet their tense decorum—Steven's and hers—and meeting it, to apprehend the uncertainty of the moment, Daniel and her father allowed themselves to gather each of them within the protective folds of their embrace. Perhaps so lighthearted a greeting might dispel the nearly imperceptible pall that glanced at their equanimity. In spite of their unease, they were braving out whatever adversity had already called them to itself.

"Come," Daniel said, while with modulated authority guiding them now to the masculine solidity of comfortable Empire chairs. The indigo-gray tints of glimmering light, a scanning motion as of the wind perceived upon the beveled window nearby, offered other comforts. "Tell us what, on such a remarkable day, has brought you to, of all places, my study."

Influenced at once by this diplomatic expression of his father's solicitude, Steven quickly recounted all that had happened in the past hour or two. He compassed his way with unflinching directness because only then could he with integrity proceed to explain.

He described to the two men the exhilaration with which he and the others had acceded to the late afternoon's promise of adventure. Forthright, he spoke of the impulse which had pushed him into so rash an enterprise—his banked capacities for a wilder courage suddenly and without warning ignited. He explained all of it, reliable man that he was and very much his own individual. Then he waited coolly, standing with her in composed alliance, while her father summoned the words that would hurry them forward to the things that they must do and not do. Her father was once again assertive Liam Maguire, roused in this moment from the lethargy that grief had imposed upon him.

"We must not tell the other guests," he said, addressing himself to Daniel as well as to Steven and her. The even timbres of his voice (a taut fluency now) as much as his silver hair and bronzed patrician features granted him a cultivated man's authenticity. "There is nothing they can do to help, at least not at the moment. And their too freely speaking of the matter might, without their intending it, only make the situation appear more grievous than it really is."

Her father further declared that they must proceed with the evening as though nothing untoward had happened. In an hour or so they must join the society of guests—twelve from that afternoon's prestigious gathering—who as weekend visitors would be the privileged recipients of Olivia Bradford's superb candle-lit dinner. With exemplary tact, he chose reasonable words meant to influence their better judgment. While doing so, he selected a supplementary language of gesture—a cultivated wave of his hand at the perimeter of brusqueness and a rugged and impatient shuffling of his Spartan frame. With the insight of a steadfast friend, he wanted to suggest that not even the wayward episode involving Tracy and Ryan should permit Daniel or Steven and her to alter the rules that required them to maintain, as much as they could, the durable harmonies of the evening.

With the proficient modulations of a man for whom behaving well must always be an active principle, he reminded her as well as Daniel and Steven of their more pressing obligations. He intended to assure the Bradfords that their return to the evening's original promises would help their cause immensely, hers and her father's, by deflecting attention from this temporary mischance involving her sister and Ryan Turner.

"I believe no harm has come to Tracy or to Ryan," he said, having urged them to go forward to the evening's festive offerings. "They are waiting out the storm somewhere, safe in a convenient place."

In any other context, she knew, her father would have regarded as intemperate so emphatic an optimism before the stern laws of risk and accident. But there in Daniel's well-appointed study, all of them held now in unresolved tension, he found optimism a worthy ally for his purposes. He meant to dispel their unease and put them in mind of the implicated blessings of earlier hours.

"This has been such a lovely day," he declared with a supreme effort of will. "I refuse to believe it will bring harm to any of us."

Tough-minded and resilient, her father was suggesting a way for them to proceed. With self-willed assurance, they must represent their useful capacities for standing with perfect equipoise before uncertainty.

Confronting this ambivalent episode involving his younger daughter and Malcolm Turner's son, her father was once more his assertive and leaderly self. All through these summer weeks, he had expressed with taciturn dignity the lonely offices of prolonged grief, imparted as they were by his inveterate discipline and by the rigorous philosophy that held anguish in, oblique and private. From time to time he had secluded himself with Tracy and with her. He was adjusting slowly to his wife's having died six months earlier and to this vacant afterward which was unmitigated by those flickering moments when he believed her to be so inexpressibly in the sun-touched shadows of the room with him and their daughters.

In this moment, he appeared to have left his grief behind him. The news of the boating misadventure had— she could see—roused the same spirit which had made him a formidable leader of Maguire industries as diverse as lumber and textiles, oil, copper and diamonds, and real estate.

"We must do everything that we can to make this evening a first-rate experience," he said. "And we must not neglect our round of golf tomorrow afternoon."

He directed these last words to Daniel and Steven.

Daniel admired her father's spirit and wanted to accommodate his brave optimism. Drawn into the shifting complexities of the hour, he intended to defer to her father's austere self-command. Steven, who with an assertive glance had already signaled his own will, also agreed that they must bring a lighthearted presence to the evening unfolding around them.

After all, a festive dinner offered as an ornament of a summer night, even a storm-laden one, requires the presence of a host and most—if not all—of his guests. Were the host to be absent, he would excite if not inquiry, the stillness of apprehension. So, accepting the good sense of her father's plan and understanding that the Coast Guard would keep them informed about the search for Ryan and Tracy, Daniel and Steven turned to the serener requirements of the evening.

As soon as he could (while he was dressing for dinner, she learned afterward), Daniel told his wife without explaining any of it that Tracy and Ryan would not be joining the dinner party. There would be time, he knew, to explain all of it later, without in that moment casting a pall upon his wife's exuberance. For in alliance with their meticulous staff she had prepared a proper celebration for their guests. He understood, of course, that even in the full knowledge of the afternoon's wayward surprise, she would have guided the evening to felicitous purposes. Olivia was, after all, a cultivated woman with sufficient experience of the world to respond sensibly to its bruising liabilities.

When she was once more alone with her father in the suite of rooms which the Bradfords had offered them during these weeks of their visit, Linda voiced her concern. She spoke quietly, not wanting her father to detect the enmity for Ryan that had risen in her ever since the hour of the boat race.

"What Ryan has done is wrong," she said. She was adjusting his bow tie just before they would make their way to the Bradfords' party. "He should be punished. His being with Tracy in this way compromises her good name."

"You mustn't worry about this matter," her father said, patting her shoulder affectionately. "Everything will turn out the way it should."

His words appeased her anticipation of the punishment which awaited Ryan. Yet she would not relinquish her look of sisterly concern. She did, however, offer her father a gentle kiss. She wanted him to know that his words pleased her.

He was going to say more. But the wind, furious and untrammeled, hurled its weight against the house as if to remind those listening that it had not yet finished with them. In mid-sentence, her father paused. Only then was she aware of how skillfully he had been disguising the more visible nuances of his apprehension. Sternly mastering whatever alarm could overtake him, he hurried forward on the momentum of new words.

"Malcolm Turner's son knows how to protect himself and protect others," he said, with a grudging respect of the young man about whom he was speaking. "Don't you worry about him or about your sister."

"But I am worried," she said. "I'm worried for her reputation. This little adventure will cost her far more than it costs Ryan."

"When all is said and done, she'll not be hurt by what's happened today," he said. "I promise you that."

Again she felt nearly solaced by this suggestion that Ryan would be duly punished because of his careless use of the day and of her sister. In the same instant, she heard music floating from the dining room and, while she and her father hurried to that festive scene, she imagined the scenarios which would call Ryan to account for his wayward conduct.

That Malcolm Turner would be involved in this meting out to his son a proper punishment, she felt certain. Just before he began dressing for dinner, her father had telephoned Ryan's father. What words they had exchanged, she did not know, because her father had closed his bedroom door before he began the conversation. She knew that the punishment would not involve scandalizing the Turner name by bringing Ryan to a court that might send him to prison. That punishment would bring scandal to Tracy, as well. Instead, she imagined, Ryan might be compelled to enter military service or to accept an indefinite exile to Europe. Whatever happened, her father would do everything to protect Tracy's name.

It was Tracy's happiness which was, before all else, the most important issue. Ever since she had come into the world, he had accorded this daughter a special, though unobtrusive, advocacy, because she needed from him a show of affectionate support far more than she herself had at any time during her girlhood. Tracy needed, as well, his careful attention and a willingness on his part to sympathize with her disappointments. Aware of her need, he had cultivated a loving and teacherly counsel that received with respectful demeanor her idiosyncratic aptitudes and that embraced always even her smallest achievements.

Year after year his fatherly acumen had harnessed his approval of Tracy's efforts to a sensible decorum. At the same time, he had maintained a care not to offer her any affection which would overshadow his love for her, his first-born daughter Linda. His was a judicious mindfulness of the obligations which every right-thinking father gladly fulfills toward each of his daughters. But he imparted toward Tracy, nonetheless, a tactful solicitude and a firmly balanced protectiveness. This intuitive collaboration with her emotional needs might, he believed, compensate for her mother's refusal to coddle or favor in any manner this second of their daughters. Although she had confessed to thinking so only once, her mother regarded Tracy as a difficult and overly sensitive girl. She wanted her to become strong-willed and self-reliant, as her older daughter was and as she herself had, long ago, learned to become. Not for her was the spiritless femininity that clings inordinately to masculine prerogative.

Whether it was this insistence that her daughters cultivate a wise assurance which influenced her muted impatience with Tracy or her association of Tracy with the grievous losses which her fate compelled her to endure, her mother never told her. So mysterious sometimes was the heart that pulsed within this soft-spoken woman whom her father had chosen as his life's companion. But when she was a self-assured girl of fifteen, her father did tell her of this problem involving her mother's relationship with Tracy. On that afternoon, during her summer recess from school, her father had called her into his study to suggest that she devote a portion of her vacation to her ten-year-old sister. For some time now he had noticed how subtly his wife distanced herself from Tracy. Because her coldness toward the child dismayed him, he occasionally reminded her of the girl's extraordinary capacities. In these conversations, he urged her, an admirable woman flawless in all respects except this, toward a finer encouragement of their younger daughter's affirming self-regard.

Her mother's subdued enmity toward Tracy had begun, he felt, on the very day that Tracy was born. For her birth made a hard delivery that had nearly cost her mother her life and thereafter impaired her once-beaming constitution. Yet only three years later, while dismissing the protests of her physicians and after with rigorous disciplines nurturing a semblance of her once-prevailing strength, she consented to carry a third child. For much of her pregnancy she accepted the imprisoning bed rest and fastidious nursing which her doctors prescribed to ensure a safe delivery. But, despite her cautious regimen, the infant was stillborn. Its death compelled within her heart new waves of bitterness, because she had lost the son for whom she and her Liam had prayed.

It was this same bitterness which, her father reluctantly admitted, had at that time hovered about his own unease. It arrived before him as if to watch the workings of his soul made visible. At that time he, too, avoided as much as he could any contact with her sister. He had consigned her, an ingratiating three-year-old, to the care of her quietly efficient governess. For this last of her pregnancies had sealed his wife's fate. Or so the most eminent of her cardiologists told her. With cautious attention to her health, she might live another decade or even two. But no longer could she, with her husband, travel as much through the world as had been their wont, nor could they socialize as often.

Not for long, though, did her father carry a secret bitterness in his heart. Only after a few weeks of his withdrawal from Tracy did he hurry to embrace her and, ever after, albeit with a more restrained approval, offer her a proper father's encouragement. As far as his busy schedule in those days allowed, he tried to compensate for the loneliness and uncertainty her mother's carefully modulated reserve wrought upon her.

She was not surprised that he forgave Tracy the first transgression to which she had willed herself. Nor was she surprised that he would impose upon Ryan a suitable penalty for misusing the younger of his daughters, whose innocent heart—he told himself—beat so tenderly. For her father, the only wonder was that Tracy had declared her independence so openly. Though there had been a show of courage in her consent to share Ryan's romantic adventure, she had journeyed into the unknown too soon. Of her hesitation about the way she should navigate her individuality beyond these fugitive hours, the immediate aftermath of her adventure would leave no doubt.

As astute as he was compassionate in his responses toward her, her father would concede that, by means of her elopement with daring young Ryan, whom she was convinced she loved profoundly, his troubled second daughter had made a tremendous leap forward to the personal autonomy she had not yet successfully negotiated. In time, with his fatherly guidance and the guidance of other caring teachers, Tracy would become strong enough to stand alone without his support and—as the Fates must allow—without Ryan. But for now, because he would see to it that Ryan hurried on to his own young destiny and because she was not yet ready to stand by herself, wholly sufficient, Tracy needed to stand with him. Quietly acknowledging that need, he would guide her toward a life far more fulfilling than the inordinate excitement which Ryan was offering her on this storm-roused day.

This, she told herself, was her father's point of view. Believing so, she consented with a poised conviviality to the Bradfords' glamorous dinner party. In the midst of loyal friends and new-found acquaintances, she felt supremely contented. She was even more pleased when Olivia Bradford whispered to her some favorable news. The full powers of the storm, its occasional rebellions notwithstanding, had merely glanced at their shores. Even more favorable, the Coast Guard, with whom Daniel and her father had been communicating all that evening, had found no evidence of any craft coming to harm. She and her father, as well as the Bradfords, were of course relieved, though still uneasy not knowing just where Ryan and Tracy might be.

A few hours later, after all the other guests had retired to their rooms in the main house or to the guest cottages nearby, she and her father sat conversing with the Bradfords within the burnished amenities of the parlor. There, each of them sipped a cordial or wine or black tea from India, while they touched upon subjects as varied as Mozart, the Summer Olympics, the latest Bentley, and Wall Street. Later, they would admit with lighthearted banter that, though they liked each other's company immensely, they had delayed retiring to their rooms because they wanted to be instantly available to receive any further news about Tracy and Ryan.

When their vigil had lasted forty-five minutes, the call from the Coast Guard came, telling them that Ryan and Tracy were safe in Bristol. They had taken shelter at an inn before the hurl of the storm could harm them.

Only then did she with her father and Steven with his parents agree that they should get some rest. The oncoming day promised to be a very busy one.

As they were making their way to their rooms, Steven turned to her father. Like them, he was very pleased to hear that Ryan and Tracy were safe.

"This problem with Ryan and Tracy is working itself out, after all," he declared with sturdy confidence.

To this remark her father, first to enter the hallway, without looking back at him offered a casual-seeming response that banked the energies of its analytic temperament. As if to consent to Steven's forecast and at the same time express a reservation, elliptical though it might be, about the idea that any problem by its own devices could work itself out, he held in check the full heft of a wise realism. Instead, her father allowed for the contingencies that sometimes shape a deed or consequence and even initiate occasionally an auspicious direction for our lives.

"Well, if it isn't going to be all right,' he said, "we can try to make it so."

4

How far from being all right everything was, to their startlement and dismay they learned the next morning. Two young Coast Guard officers, Jeremy Britten and Erik Douglas, from boyhood days fishing pals of Steven and since early summer venture-rousing friends of Ryan, had accelerated rather than merely accompanied Ryan's and Tracy's prompt and discreet return from Bristol. In a private conference the summary of which she learned from Olivia afterward, they quietly informed her father and Malcolm

Turner, who had an hour earlier arrived from his summer home in Nantucket, about the wayward episode into which Ryan had entangled Tracy as well as himself.

Jeremy and Erik began by speaking of Ryan with that ingrained respect and admiration which capable men accord prowess and aggressiveness. With a flash of recognition that the potency of Ryan's young daring was not unlike their own wild comfort with adventurous chance, they praised his expertise, coolly rendered, in outracing the storm. They also mentioned favorably his clearheaded success in bringing Tracy to the sheltering amenities of Bristol Inn. More than once they remarked upon the courtesy and equanimity that never failed him, not even when confronted by the angry scene that had erupted at the inn early that morning.

But they said all these things as a preface (shrewdly calculated, her father bethought himself later) to all the other words that needed saying. Duty-bound to stringent regulations, they had to report to Tracy's father and to Ryan's, too, that Ryan Turner, riding on the cusp of a storm-bruised day, had brought himself and Tracy dangerously near the path of a scandal.

"Without meaning to, he's got himself and the young lady into a bit of a tangle," Jeremy explained.

His magisterial height and hard blue eyes transformed wind-burned physicality into someone commanding. As he met directly the probing inquiry of the two men before him, he was all the while measuring the weight of precisely chosen words upon the taut self-containment of her dignified father and upon the subdued concern, as genuine though without the tautness, of Daniel.

"But he's a first-rate fellow all the same," Erik interposed, quickly speaking on Ryan's behalf.

The older men noticed, and were to mention later, his ruddy confidence and that of his cohort. They noticed, too, how lightly cynicism influenced their dutiful attentiveness. Tough-minded, they could gather still the plausible words meant to exonerate their friend's questionable intentions.

What had happened at the inn at eight o'clock that morning, as though the unexpected episode, as swift as it was rancorous, were coiling intricacies of malice about Tracy and Ryan, nearly compromised the Maguires' good name. Having outraced the hurl of the storm on the sea, these two rebellious individuals had in the roiling flare of the preceding afternoon presented themselves at the inn as a newly-married couple.

In that hour the assailing wind was rising against the white clapboard eaves of the large colonial house (carefully restored and retaining still its original imagery as a sea-captain's property). The pulsive rain thrashed across sky-blown waves of summer-fragrant trees, a profusion of symmetries all plum and peach and almond flowering italic and sovereign over the wide expanse of emerald greenery. Wondrously in wind and rain did that wind-sown splendor glide and ascend and scale storm-crossed altitudes. At the same time the frantic rain lashed the graveled path hurrying away from fertile woodlands behind the house. Not only the rain but the sweep and whirl and swell of wind kept battering the inn's columns and eaves, gables and windows and sloping roof-top. Cobalt-blue wicker chairs were toppling across a velvet-soft lawn before croquet hoops and mallet and ball. Conservative guests, roused in the lift and surge and liability of a momentary reprieve from humdrum routine, hastened with their children to indoor comforts.

Perhaps it was the rush and swerve and startlement of so kinetic a scene that lent a plausibility to Ryan and Tracy's being in their unanticipated arrival all that they said they were— young marrieds from the Bradford estate eluding a stormy bay's rising powers. Or possibly it was the chance happening that Mr. and Mrs. Collins, keepers of the inn, were so held to the worry of the storm and intent upon battening down the large house and grounds from late afternoon's incoming betrayals that they, as well as their staff and guests, could at first offer scant attention to Ryan and Tracy's arrival. There was a naturalness, shaping its own spontaneity, to their being suddenly there and they also hastening to escape the storm's brute treacheries. It was that, perhaps, which made them plausible. Or, more likely, Ryan's affability and directness quickly won the Collinses' approval and Tracy's demureness pleased.

Whether it was all of these things or only some of them or one more than any other that influenced the innkeeper and his wife, as well as their staff and guests, to accept Ryan and Tracy as wholly authentic, neither she nor her father ever learned. Nor did Tracy tell when she described to her and their father the specific unfolding of that fateful day.

What words first described their time at the inn, Ryan and Tracy's, were an elliptical translation of all that had happened there glancing at the harsh truth through subtlety and indirection. Those words belonged to the two Coast Guardsmen, Erik and Jeremy, who meant with calculated understatement to justify their venture-rousing friend and his warm-hearted young lady. As tersely as they could and as impassively, they informed her father and Daniel that Ryan and Tracy, pretending to be married, had brought an angry scene upon themselves, as well as the ugly threat of being detained or arrested.

That the two Coast Guardsmen were willing to reveal this much, and more, of what others were calling the young couple's subversion of public morality reflected the diplomatic compromise they had made with the sheriff of

Bristol. As if they were crafty strategists negotiating in the spirit of truce or détente or apparent reparation, they were gaining far more for Ryan and Tracy than they had permitted themselves to forfeit. What they were forfeiting, though only to her father and to Daniel, was their silence about the episode. Leagued momentarily with the innkeepers, they had by pledging away that silence held at bay the unexpected adversary who had threatened to expose Tracy and Ryan to public disgrace.

In this subtle partnership with the Coast Guardsmen, it was the keepers of the inn, Bartley and Maureen Collins, who were essential to the swift efforts they had all made to protect the young couple from so stern and precipitate an adversary as Warren Thompson. Within the first hours of seeing them, the Collinses decided they liked the "idea" of Ryan and Tracy, who were so romantic and life-loving. As they themselves had once done, these two extraordinary people were making their way without the consent of their parents. (When Ryan explained his and Tracy's situation to them, he took care to mention all those concerned with a calm and respectful deference.)

What a lift to the spirit it was, even in that first fleet witness after they had been called away momentarily from the business of securing the imperiled house from the rising storm, to come approve the two strangers hurrying still out of the distance toward the beleaguered inn. The Collinses had been alerted to the surprise of them by their goodhearted secretary and sometime clerk Mrs. Reed, who had kept watch at the desk while others worked to protect the house from the storm. Watching, she saw from the southeast corner the two of them hastening with agile fluency along the wind-torn road that stretched away from the harbor and met, coiling and accurate, the graveled path that would guide them to the waiting colonial inn.

By that time the Collinses were standing within the burnished stability of the reception area ready to greet them and, greeting, scan their healthy glow before returning to the task of safeguarding the house from the weather. It was wonderful and mysterious and italic to see them so suddenly there and passing on their way to them with supple ease through the white glistening portico sinuous about the house, its columns and pillars hand-hewn and "southernized." Their brightness passed as well along the spacious entry hall by limestone hearth and Shaker child's chair and cauldrons of brass filled with cedar-scented firewood.

Confidently arriving, they paused beneath rafters pendulous with antique baskets and pomegranate medallion quilts and sprigs of orange-hued bittersweet. Then, their bearings quietly affirmed, they continued on to the polished-oak reception desk. Luminous behind it against the wall, a brocaded green tapestry carried as its

Gaelic salutation an invocation and spirited wish and affecting beneficence: *Caed Mille Failte*—one hundred thousand welcomes.

Afterward, resourceful Ryan and amenable Tracy refreshed themselves, secluded and liberal in the comforting pleasures of their room. Then, bathed and contented, they came to the affable society of the candle-lit parlor to share with other guests their experience of art and music, sport and adventure and travel. Always they melded their language to enthusiasm as fluent and vital as the occasions in which, stirred by the press of desire or venturous aptitude or activity memorable and enhancing, they had consummated its privileges. Later, too, when they enjoyed a festive meal within the colorful traceries of the dining room, they were in those public hours responsive to the others there with them in random alliance happily met at the splendid table where, mutual and expansive, they found themselves together.

That evening, of the thirty-two guests residing at the spacious inn, seven or eight enjoying dinner with them were inspired (so the Collinses later told Olivia Bradford) by Ryan's and Tracy's heartening anecdotes. Ryan told them of his hunting red stag in Patagonia. He also spoke of tracking the elusive whitetail buck in the pinyan-juniper forests of Montana and of cycling through the Chang Tang region of the Tibetan Plateau in China. Tracy recounted her visits to France and to British Columbia. She also spoke of skiing in Vermont and of flying with her father in a Curtiss PW-8. In turn the other guests also shared narratives about their own explorations scanning the kinetic surprise that was one's self extemporaneous in the world, negotiating possibility. They, all of them there together, were a most compatible society. If not proven confederates, they were potential allies recognizing in each other correspondent energies.

What a lift it was, the Collinses were to agree, as they summarized to Olivia afterward the complete surprise of that day. What a spark it was, igniting their own memories of early passion that surged beyond the ordinary measures of joy, to notice the love in Ryan Turner's eyes as he cast his heated glance upon Tracy. From time to time and with decorous modesty, she met that glance, so that everyone there observing them at the table believed them to be an ideal married couple. While moving about the tables to supervise their staff's care of the guests, Mr. and Mrs. Collins observed them as well. They found themselves especially pleased that chance had brought to their inn, as though they were a gift or godsend for a stormy evening, these two vibrant persons who had influenced a few wearying and ominous hours to become one of life's happier occasions.

5

Ryan and Tracy had planned all of it together, this game of pretending to be married which would draw them into an adventure of their own making. With restless anticipation, her sister consented to whatever devices she with Ryan might impose upon its wayward subtexts. That, in these several weeks of being guests of the Bradfords, they had come in secret to know each other well was all to the good—the good, that is, of their liberated purposes. They were enclosed, though, within a group of their peers. From time to time they were aware as well of Steven and her dutifully watching from a distance while allowing all of them, seven or eight, a provisional freedom. Carefully observed, Ryan and Tracy could claim a promising intimacy only by availing themselves of the enshadowed path or unobtrusive alcove or sequestering arbor.

At first they had to pretend that they were attracted primarily to their team of friends and not to each other particularly. Whenever casual occasions or summer celebrations called them to join the group, they behaved toward one another as nothing more than courteous allies. Yet with Ryan even obliquely, Tracy regarded their proximity as an extraordinary hour. Theirs was a nearness that suggested. It became a subtler emphasis receiving togetherness as a union of themselves alone even when attended by well-bred girls and hardy youths and personable chaperones.

It was thrilling to be with each other even obliquely, while, with their exuberant friends and dutiful chaperones still there as an affable necessity, they swam in the Bradfords' cantilevered pool where the blue-green waters flowed as if by magic into the Atlantic. On other inspiriting days they went cantering along the soft turf of that portion of the Bradfords' estate given over to a capacious horse farm. There, while riding a tawny-colored Welsh Cob or an Austrian Haflinger with chestnut body and flaxen mane, they sometimes jumped fences. Their hands and arms stretched forward to follow the movement of the horse's head and neck. Adept riders, each of them remained perfectly still and correctly balanced over the horse, thereby leaving the horse free to jump athletically over the fence. On other days they sailed over Newport waters, found themselves exuberant at a county fair, and—as a foursome who included Steven and her—rode in a De Havilland D.H.50 which Steven and Ryan co-piloted.

Then there came those times when they were alone. They would most often meet within a thatched-roof summer cottage which stood a half-mile from the Bradfords' home, yet on their property none the less. With its gable detailing, the cottage recalled the pavilion spread of a Japanese house. Far more spacious than a conventional cottage, this guest house enjoyed a sheltered location. All around it were full-grown evergreens, a Momi fir, red cedars, mugho pines, and Japanese hollies. White-tinged Japanese painted fern highlighted a shaded corner outside the cottage.

Here, because the house was currently unoccupied, Ryan made love to Tracy.

Twice, he made love to her within a wisteria-covered gazebo which a small bridge linked to a pond. The delicate whiteness of Iris ensata played against the dark waters of the rock-lined pond.

He was devising the episode by which, in a setting more secure than a gazebo or a cottage where a gardener or groundskeeper might interrupt their lovemaking, they could consummate their love without any chance of being discovered. Being of his class, she meant far more to him than the occasional girls who had from time to time satisfied his sexual needs. He wanted to protect her from the harm of gossip or from the penalties invoked by a narrow community. For him, Tracy was an altogether different experience. The two of them were, he told himself, in mind and spirit already married.

So it was through this idea—a convincing assertion of their bond with each other—that he came to persuade her of the rightness of his plan. At a picturesque inn within the secluded seaport of Bristol, they would—in fragrant privacies and without the Church's approving seal or any other legal document permitting them—celebrate once more the marriage of their bodies to one another. At first they would register as the husband and wife their own personal laws made them. That they, by so appearing, would attain a comfortable marriage room for the union of their souls and bodies, even as they subverted narrow convention and protected Tracy from the public's accusing eyes, would serve well to enhance their mutual pleasure.

"How clever you are," Tracy said just before kissing him once more, exhilarated and breathless.

"There are many ways to have an adventure," he told her. His full, sensual lips caressed now the exquisite lobe of her right ear. "We'll wait awhile and find the proper day for this one to begin."

They had to wait merely a week. The Bradfords' grand summer party provided the ideal occasion for launching their rebellious flight. Ryan's challenging Steven to a boat race over restless waters initiated an adequate scenario. It became a lighthearted enterprise for stealing away from familial watchfulness. But the storm interfered with the swift unfolding of his plan to elude temporarily the Bradfords and Liam Maguire and, at a solacing inn, to enjoy a few blissful hours with this loving young woman for whom his passion had amply grown. They'd imagined that they would return, sated and inspirited, to explain that they had merely been sailing the exciting race that he and Steven had agreed to wager. Even when the storm rose to mar his plan to go back to the Bradfords by early evening, Ryan did not waver.

Although he rightly calculated, with his cynical awareness of the world, that the randomness of things might gainsay his efforts, he permitted himself to imagine that he and Tracy could, once they had smoothly arrived at Bristol Inn, telephone the Bradfords to declare that all was well and that the inn was happily providing them attractive shelter within the propriety of separate rooms. (They would be wearing the gold wedding bands he'd won in a poker game while he was vacationing in Buenos Aires. He had won them from an exiled Frenchman, a corrupt banker trafficking now in the black market.)

But, the storm assailing Bristol's telephone lines, Ryan could not make the call that would mollify the startled authority they had left behind them. Nor could he return with Tracy on the evening of that day. Both the Coast Guard and local police were to come in search of them, complicating his deftly constructed scenario. Yet, in spite of them all, he and Tracy still achieved their love, enjoying in a secluded room at the inn a union of their bodies and spirit and wilder nature.

So Tracy was to tell her, referring to her experience of those hours as the best happiness of her life thus far.

6

But early the following day a rancorous scene dispelled whatever solace the evening had granted them. For Warren Thompson, the sheriff of the town, had come to the inn searching for a young man and an even younger girl who, when caught on the storm-roused waters of Narragansett Bay, might have by luck or quick wit or a lithe acumen found their way to land and to adequate shelter. Having, during the previous afternoon's rising turbulence, been alerted by the Coast Guard about the missing pair, Sheriff Thompson—at some peril to himself—had been scouting about the houses nearest to the water, until toppled tree-limbs in the middle of primary roads and street-floods from the lashing rains deterred his search. Then in the morning, after the storm had ended and safe passages, because of the work of vigorous crews, were beginning to be restored, he (still searching) had come to the Collinses' inn. There, he discovered that Ryan and Tracy had registered as a married couple and had spent the night together.

Sheriff Thompson was a gaunt, stern man of forty. The bronze of his skin was a summer emphasis for so personal a reality as his gray-black crew cut and cold, brown eyes, as well as his aquiline nose and tight-lipped self-command. His tall, rangy frame rose to an extraordinary six-foot, four inches and enhanced his military bearing. There were within him subtly visible traces of rigorous judgments and lacerating disciplines, of unflinching severity and a brooding cynicism. In spite of his hardened demeanor, the Collinses liked him. Bartley and Maureen had capacities for glimpsing, a little at least, into the bruised soul or fragmented spirit or battered heart. Their affection was also inspired by his being true to the Spartan code that, they felt, must have helped him make sense of things.

His parents had been loyal friends of Mrs. Collins' aunt and had, before she died, spent many afternoons or evenings visiting with her at the inn and even at times helping her in the very busy summer season. As if fostering their own variant of this friendship, Warren and his wife had stayed at the inn during the first few anniversaries of their marriage. They were favorably disposed toward the kind and long-widowed woman and toward the equally hardworking Collinses. How happy Warren and Louise were in those days. (So the Collinses from time to time later recalled.) The young sheriff and his wife were conscious, while savoring present joys, of the bright promises their tomorrows held for them.

Afterward, they were happiest when they had their first child, a healthy boy. By the time he was nine years old, this son called forth an earlier imagery of his father's cool, level gaze and his supple physicality. Already, he had acquired an affinity for the tests of courage and stamina his father was wont to devise on his behalf, the better to shape properly his masculine powers. Some of those powers the boy was discovering through soldierly marching formations and calisthenics and swimming. Habits like precision drills became ingrained, addictive mastery.

But then everything changed. The boy, Warren's namesake and in subtle ways something of his alter ego, a second self growing into a parallel identity, died of pneumonia right after his eleventh birthday. The child had taken ill when his father, heedless of Louise's cautious petitioning not to go, brought the boy to his first experience of hunting rabbits inside the autumn rawness of the Bristol woods. After the boy died, flushed with fever and, to the last, fighting the strange, breathtaking malady, the two of them—Warren and Louise—were never to each other the same. Whatever brightness they together had once achieved had, with the boy, burnt out its light.

Bitter and grief-struck and guilty, Warren could not locate within himself a strategy that would help his Louise to see how lost he was. Instead, with tough-skinned taciturnity and longer hours at his work as the sheriff of Bristol, he salvaged the exterior part of himself that had not been destroyed. But he had no art or will to find the words that could guide her into his soul. There were between them no intimate conversations that would help her to recall how elated the boy had always been to hone, with his father's coaching, early aptitudes for fishing and boxing, soccer and swimming and gymnastics. Each of them had been a test and validation of his emerging prowess and a promise that he, too, would one day be as tall and sturdy and knowing as his father.

Without being offered any of those words as his way to call out his grief to her, she began to regard him as a stranger, arbitrary and inhuman. All his familiar masculine responses that had seemed protective now appeared to her new eyes as an insidious method of controlling not only the boy's life, but her own as well. Again and again he had deferred to his will alone. Her will had been an ancillary volition meant to be, in relation to him, merely feminine and assenting.

Eventually, he saw in her accusing sullenness flashes of contempt and hatred and a dark refusal to forgive him, even were he—months after the boy's dying—to find the necessary, penitent phrases. So they turned away from each other, except for the few times, raging with desire and loneliness and despair, he took her by force. On those nights, Warren Thompson experienced through his mastering potency the fiercer ecstasy that comes to those men whose confident bodies are roused with keener appetite in the very act of dominating frail and resisting loveliness.

Yet, in spite of her disdain and her fear of his primitive fury, she found her hatred falling away from her. From time to time and only by chance now, she met his haunted gaze upon her. It was a gaze as well of tender love and of mute yearning. His intelligent brow was usually caught in a frown. Now the full lips whose pressing touch upon her own had once brought her immense pleasure curved downward in a grimace, a sign she read as his raw and wounding self-hatred.

Because she felt that he could no longer in any of the essential ways solace her, she left him five months after their son had died. She returned at first to her parents' home in Dover, Delaware, and eventually, after the divorce which through his lawyer he protested, she found her way back to a less complicated happiness. By then she had met again, while in a wholly new way perceiving, a gentle fellow from her high school days who had become a dedicated veterinarian and lived a solitary bachelor's existence. He'd never moved past the emotional alliance which they had in an earlier, platonic season made.

It was after they'd married that Warren Thompson, bereft and angry, understood clearly, as though it were a prophecy his own actions had delivered, all his happiness was now behind him.

On that sun-tinted July morning two years later when, at the Collins' inn, he confronted Ryan and Tracy,

Warren Thompson was indeed a bitter man. The sight of them together at breakfast, rapt in each other as if transported still by desire wakened and fulfilled, roused in him a despairing envy of their happiness. That same ease and contentment, he and Louise had once enjoyed. In the beginning, the love they'd experienced together had become their own symmetry. With him, she'd consented to a carnality that was for body and mind and spirit a solacing excitement. The painful truth that at the last he'd taken by force the soft pleasures of her body he believed by law were his to possess made him despair of his fate all over again in the instant he observed Ryan and Tracy. Quite apart from his envy of their happiness and his grief over his personal loss—and yet inciting his anger just as keenly—was the goading thought that, from a privileged class, they believed they were their own law, above restrictive codes and admonishing conventions.

Whether it was that thought more even than his quiet despair that influenced Warren's hostility toward Ryan and Tracy, Mrs. Collins would not allow herself to guess. She remembered only the brooding manner in which, at the threshold of the crowded dining room, he watched while her husband, without inviting the concern of any other guest, made his way to Ryan and Tracy. In cordial harmony with the requirements of the moment, she stood beside Sheriff Thompson as he sighted lovely Tracy with venturous Ryan. By this time her husband had quietly approached them.

They were a most romantic couple, seated as they were by a spacious window that overlooked the tranquil, iridescent bay. Sailboats in the distance and swimmers not far from shore were already navigating the luminous waters. Mrs. Collins observed how the sight of them brought to Warren's tension a face whose chiseled profile suggested, almost imperceptibly, the intricacies of anguish. As if it were a casual gesture, she drew him, while slipping her hand gently through the curve of his rugged arm, away from the threshold to the privacy of Bartley's office. She did not want any guests to connect the sheriff's pausing there on the rim of the room—to search out, perhaps, before going urgently forward to them—to this romantic, young couple whom she and her husband regarded still as ideal, whether or not they were married.

"You've broken the law," Sheriff Thompson said, confronting Ryan and Tracy with accusation stark and threatening the moment they'd entered Bartley's office. "You've lied about being married and have had carnal relations with each other."

Ryan comforted at once a startled Tracy with a gallant pressure of his hand upon her own. He positioned himself in front of her and thereby protected her from this unexpected adversary. Then he moved forward to face

Warren Thompson with unflinching directness.

"We've done no wrong," he asserted coolly, "and, as for being married, we are—in soul and spirit and body. We need no legal paper to tell us so."

"That's not the way we think around here," Warren said. "But it's a good way to get yourselves arrested."

"Whatever has happened between us concerns ourselves and nobody else."

It was then that the Collinses, Bartley and Maureen, noticed Warren's hand drawing from his windbreaker a metallic jangle of handcuffs. Quickly they stepped between the sheriff and this youth they had grown to admire.

"Let it alone, Warren," Bartley said, the rich timbres of his Irish inflections respectful, yet counseling a friend nonetheless. "Let it be. These are fine young people."

The sheriff, without looking at him, for his sullen eyes were all the while fixed in appraisal of Ryan, resisted the burly innkeeper's words.

"You're out of line, Bart," he said. "There's been a violation of the law here."

"These are fine young people," the strong-minded innkeeper declared once more. His echoing thought was another way for Warren to see.

"They've brought harm to no one," Maureen added.

The crisp fluency of her voice drew Warren's attention now to her calm and fetching demeanor.

"If you carry this further than it need be carried, you will bring harm to us and to our inn"

Perhaps it was their addressing him in the name of the long friendship they'd shared with him that tempered the harshness of Sheriff Thompson's judgment.

Or perhaps it was the happy chance that, at this moment precisely, wise Mrs. Reed appeared. Her silver hair and brown, gentle eyes; her delicate nose; and her mouth and chin granted her large, motherly girth a benevolent dignity. She was ushering into the room the two Coast Guardsmen, Jeremy Britten and Erik Douglas. Several hours earlier, they'd located Ryan's boat in the harbor. After verifying that Ryan Turner and Tracy Maguire were safely housed at the inn, Jeremy had telephoned the Bradfords that all was well. Then, without disturbing their friend Ryan and his young lady, the two Coast Guardsmen had told Bartley that they would, out of deference to Mr. Maguire and Mr. Bradford, accompany Ryan and Tracy home.

But first they must respond to an urgent call from their commanding officer directing them, just then, to assist an elderly widow. That good woman was stranded in her flooded cottage on a graveled road the wind-driven rains had nearly washed away. She needed safe passage to the inn, where the Collinses would prepare a room for her. So, having now returned, delivering the grateful widow to the reception desk, the two Coast Guardsmen proceeded to join Bartley and Maureen. Subtly, they shaped a plan for the young couple which would, in the sheriff's eyes, bring them to the equivalent of a stern tribunal or a judicious hearing.

Perhaps it was the Coast Guardsmen's timely arrival which influenced the sheriff most of all. And possibly it was, a little at least, Warren Thompson's ambivalent regard of the two young romantics which tempered his hard will. He had a grudging respect for Ryan's manly directness and a pulsing awareness of Tracy's extraordinary beauty and her refinement. He noticed how quietly she had recovered her poise while mooring it to its own, natural demureness. She and Ryan expressed a passionate love not so very unlike the one which he and Louise had in their best years known together.

Whatever truth hid itself within these possibilities, the Collinses, upon retiring to their rooms that evening and even in later reminiscence with Olivia, could not with certainty declare to each other. They simply acknowledged that the plan they had quietly devised, in league with the quick-wittedness of the Coast Guardsmen, may have been the catalyst which saved Ryan and Tracy from a scandal. Warren, whose rigid principles needed to be satisfied, agreed—though with some reluctance—that Erik and Jeremy would accompany Miss Maguire and Mr. Turner back to the home of their hosts, the upright Bradfords.

There, they would duly inform her father and Malcolm Turner of what the sheriff deemed to be the young couple's wrongdoing. Having heard only good things of Mr. Maguire and of Mr. Turner, he was reasonably convinced that, as solid citizens, they would bring upon Ryan and Tracy a proper punishment.

7

"You've had an exciting weekend," Malcolm Turner asserted with casual ambivalence.

He was closely observing this bright arrogance before him—- this complicated Ryan who was his only heir. The cool light of the room revealed that Malcolm's muscular physique was finely honed and, at forty-six, impressive still. That morning she—Linda Maguire, the conscientious sister of the reckless Tracy—scanned Malcolm Turner's rugged features and found in them the nearly imperceptible scar buried across the left side of his face. It was a fading emblem of the grievous war wound he had sustained in battle on the sea against turbulent Spain at the close of the nineteenth century. The radiance of that same light noticed his curly gray hair and thick, dapper mustache. His was a diplomatic emphasis of individuality that still maintained its own laws and privileges.

"But you have forgotten your obligations to the name you carry and to the well-being of this young lady."

They were standing directly before him now, his prepossessing son with her fair-skinned sister. Two in so italic an alliance might have, had the circumstance been apt and permissible, represented to her quiet observation an extraordinary romantic ideal. They were standing as if poised and united before him in the Bradfords' main parlor and within the resourceful witness of her father and of Daniel Bradford, as well as of Steven and her. These reliable fathers had agreed to see the wayward couple minutes after exchanging cordial, parting words with the quick-witted Coast Guardsmen. During this meeting with the Coast Guardsmen, she and Steven had brought Tracy and Ryan, dazzling still even while waiting on the rim of uncertainty, to the east wing of the house—apart from any chance encounter with the affable guests with whom Olivia would later that day be leaving for an afternoon's excursion to Newport's summer-festival atmosphere.

Only after that meeting with the Coast Guardsmen did they accompany Tracy and Ryan to the parlor. At this time, Daniel, Steven, and she remained as anchoring influences over Malcolm and her father, as well as over Tracy and Ryan. They had come with modulated aptitudes to mediate, if need be, the tenser liabilities of this meeting.

"We had an afternoon's adventure, sir," Ryan explained while keenly measuring the weight of his words upon the three older men.

From comments that he had made to her and to Steven in the weeks just passed, he had made it clear that he respected these men. He respected their self-command and their achievements. With his pragmatic calculations for measuring the heft of a person's character, he perceived them as authentic. Their quests drew them always to the wider world—-to its perilous enterprises and its manifold rewards. It was in that turbulent and uncertain world, in territories not unlike those over which his father and the other men prevailed, where he intended to activate whatever larger capacities waited to be summoned from within himself.

She imagined that he understood these men well. His was a youth's unobtrusive empathy which recognized in them his own advocacy of brave and rigorous explorations. Because of that, he held himself in clipped and pertinent understatement while standing with Tracy before them. Nor did he betray his conviction that he and Tracy, expressing freely in a summery room so natural an ardor as their passion for each other, had done no wrong.

"We found the inn while the storm was becoming dangerous," he said, his matter-of-factness mooring itself to a temperate assurance. "But no harm has come to either of us."

Her father, disappointed in this casual-seeming viewpoint, quickly demurred.

"What happened at the inn, your being in that room together as a married couple, is a dark blame upon your character," he said. "You've compromised Tracy's honor and your own as well."

"Oh, Father, you don't know how it is with us," her sister hurried to explain. Her voice was matter of fact and assertive. "Ryan and I are in love and will be in love for the rest of our lives."

She paused before the thought that would help them to see even more clearly the way it was between Ryan and her.

"I don't believe that my being at the inn with Ryan was wrong," she said. "But if you gentlemen think it was, then we're willing to face the consequences."

With understated solidarity, the three older men glanced at each other. Her sister's words had obviously pleased them.

"In that case," Malcolm said, "our meeting should go very well."

He was speaking for her father and for Daniel and Steven, as well as for himself. No sooner had he made his remark, than the four of them accompanied Tracy and Ryan into Daniel's study.

At this time, she excused herself because (she imagined) Steven and her father would not want her to be involved any further in a scene which was already fraught with many tensions. That this private conference—with its legal underpinnings—would involve not only the two fathers, but also Daniel and Steven as judicious mediators once more roused her expectation that both Ryan and her sister were going to be punished. They had broken the rules and needed to be punished.

For the next hour, she assisted Olivia's able gardeners in the careful transfer of camellias from the conservatory to a southerly corner of the garden nearest the main house. There, for the rest of the summer, the camellias would thrive within an alliance of full sun and dappled, occasional shade.

When she had completed that task, she found herself especially pleased that she had brought both a poised calm and a rational purpose to what might have loomed as an uneasy time of waiting. Only then did she permit herself to return to the main house and to the parlor that stood as if observing the closed door to Daniel's study.

In the first few minutes that she sat waiting, she could hear excited voices emanating from the study. No sooner was her curiosity roused in a new way, than Chapman came into the parlor. Bowing as he passed her, he hurried on to the study to deliver the tray of champagne which Daniel had apparently requested.

She rose from her chair slowly, because she was trying to fit together the fragments of the puzzling scenario unfolding before her. In that very instant, right after opening the door of the study to receive Chapman with the tray of wine, Olivia Bradford—noticing her—hurried forward.

Daniel had called his wife to the room twenty minutes earlier. He as well as those four others with whom he had been conferring in his study wanted to share their news with her. Malcolm had already telephoned the good news to his wife, who had stayed behind in Nantucket to orchestrate a convivial day with six of their New York friends. So Olivia explained, as she invited her to join what promised to be a moment all of them would remember.

"It has all been arranged, my dear," she said. "Ryan and Tracy will be married in two weeks."

Only by remaining very still could she find her way to what she hoped was an acceptable response.

"I can't believe that my father would agree to such a marriage," she said. "Tracy isn't ready to take that step. Nor is Ryan."

"But your father and Malcolm won't have it any other way," Olivia said. "They want them to be married. They've wanted it for a long time."

"My father never mentioned it to me."

"He never mentioned it to anyone else apparently, except Malcolm," Olivia said. "From time to time, the two of them have had serious discussions about the possibility of uniting the Maguires and the Turners through Tracy and Ryan. Their weekend adventure convinced your father and Malcolm that the time was just right for a marriage between the two."

"It isn't right," she protested. "They're being rewarded for having done wrong."

"Is it so wrong to fall in love?" Olivia asked. "You should see how happy Tracy and Ryan are. Everything has worked in their favor."

Linda frowned, unable to conceal her angry dismay.

Noticing her unease, Olivia patted her shoulder gently before offering her some motherly counsel.

"Be happy for your sister," she said. "Be happy that she is happy. Her dream has come true, and that is a very rare thing, indeed."

"I want her to be happy," she assured her. "But I'm still very worried. Ryan may not be the man who can bring her a lasting happiness."

"She thinks he will," Olivia said. "She's ready to take a leap into the unknown, and that is all that really matters."

"Perhaps you are right," she agreed diplomatically. "I'll hope for her sake that you are."

"Of course I am right," Olivia declared while smiling. She sounded brisk and lighthearted. "I know when two people are very much in love. I have only to look at Ryan and Tracy together, and I know."

They were moving now toward the study where—she saw in the distance—Malcolm, Daniel, Steven and her father were already raising their glasses to the young couple who would soon be married.

She would join them in their conviviality. She would smile and even laugh and, if there were songs to be sung, she would sing. She would embrace her sister and embrace Ryan, too. She was prepared to accept him, because to do otherwise would betray her bitter memory of his playing with her affection. For a few weeks, while she and Steven were in his company, he had quietly seduced her with the intensity of his casual gaze and the smoothness of his words. Then, when she had begun to give him her heart, he had turned away from her the instant he met her sister.

Toward him, she too would be casual and as friendly as the rules allowed. But never would she forgive him for having played so carelessly with her desire.

PART TWO

THE COMPLEXITIES OF SEDUCTION

1

Desire had overtaken Tracy. It made her a recipient of its pleasures. It rendered her a servant of its maladies. Too often now, desire clouded her understanding of the self that she had always known so well. No longer did she feel comfortable with the decisions that she was making about her life. No longer did she easily recognize in her mind's eye or in any convenient mirror the vaguely apprehensive young woman who stared back at her. There was insolence in that apprehension, and defiance, too. There was also a hardened willfulness that conjoined its powers with a plan to avenge herself against her husband's betrayal. Despite his deception, despite his subterfuge, trickery, and serial acts of adultery, she still loved Ryan. What woman would not love him? He was the prince of happiness, the bearer of ecstasy, the god of daytime exhilaration and of nighttime sensuality. He was all of these men and more than these men. He was her obsession. He was her rescuer. He was her lifeline.

So she believed and, believing so, she made herself his prisoner and a prisoner as well of her desire for him.

Because she needed him, because in subtle ways he had lost interest in always being there to rescue her, and because of her willingness to learn once again how to rescue herself, she had devised a plan that might bring him back to her—faithful and attentive and amorous. Their being together even now as an apparently loyal and happily married couple was all to the good—the good that translated its aims through her careful planning. Blind Chance favored her cause. It was exactly that, Blind Chance, that allowed her to make a friend of Ethan Lonergan, who happened to be the husband of Ava Lonergan—the beautiful woman to whom Ryan had given for at least this season all the sensual love and all the fervor of his carefree heart. Seven weeks ago, on the thirtieth of July, a fateful Thursday in this uneasy year of nineteen-hundred-twenty-five, she and Ethan began their own sensual adventure. During that same week, Ryan and Ava were attending important business conferences in New York. They had taken separate flights, but they were both staying at The Ritz-Carlton—discreetly, in separate suites.

That she—Tracy Maguire Turner—had begun a love affair with the husband of Ryan's latest paramour gave to the pleasure of her rebellion a jolt of exciting energy. Her affair with Ethan became an adrenaline rush. It quickened her spirit. It revived her belief in her romantic powers. It convinced her that, at the age of twenty-three, she was a more knowing partner for a man who was willing to share with her not only his well-honed sensuality, but also and often his urgent desire and sometimes his authentic love. For the five years of her marriage to Ryan, she had played the roles that Ryan wanted her to play. For him and for all the other estimable persons of their class, she had been the elegant debutante. She had excelled as well in the role of a sophisticated hostess at the extravagant parties that she and Ryan created for the admiration and exhilaration of their many friends. In the annual Newport regattas, she had been his adept sailing cohort. She had proved herself a savvy co-pilot whenever they flew their de Havilland DH.50 from Boston to New York. She had fused her daring and her skill with his accomplished maneuvering whenever they skied in Lausanne or made the rigorous climb up Mount Washington in New Hampshire or raced their swift, gold-coated Palominos across the wide span of the horse trail a quarter of a mile behind her father's Newport mansion and still a part of his property. In all these adventures, she had been a loyal partner to Ryan. She had also been the patient wife who always looked the other way whenever Ryan strayed from his sporadic fidelity to her.

Now it was her turn to prevail in this complicated game of seduction. Now it was her time to choose a partner who would equal and even exceed Ryan's prowess as a lover. This man would have to be as handsome as Ryan and as exciting. Her newly discovered need of him would become as predominant as it was intense. To stir Ryan's surprise and his jealousy, she needed an extraordinary man.

It pleased her that Ethan Lonergan fulfilled so admirably her desire for a new, extraordinary partner.

During these seven weeks that had so swiftly unfolded their contrived and ambivalent episodes, she and Ethan had become more than friends. He was her vigorous and sullen lover. He was also manipulative, scheming, and dangerous. She found his coming into her life both timely and ironic. It was timely because he fulfilled in extraordinary and unorthodox ways her need of a young, handsome man who could play with conviction the intricate scenario that she had devised to revive her husband's interest in her and to rouse his jealousy. Ethan's unanticipated appearance in her life was ironic because her upright and conservative father, inspired by an annual surge of altruism, was the instrument for their first meeting at a lavish party at a Newport country club that celebrated her father's birthday. Learning of Ethan's fall from grace in an earlier year because of a Wall Street investment scandal, her father wanted to be the guardian of his rehabilitation, the agent of his reconciliation with his estimable father, and the manager of his comeback. Though he had sullied his reputation with scandal, Ethan came with the right credentials. His lawyerly aptitudes and his savvy comprehension of the corporate world made her father's endorsement of him both pragmatic and discerning.

Ethan's relationship with her engendered altogether different episodes. She had not anticipated that she would fall in love with him with such passionate and possessive intensity. Reluctantly, she admitted to herself (though not to anyone else) that, when she first met him, she had been ready for a love affair. But she had not planned to fall in love with him. That she had fallen in love with him despite his surly willfulness surprised her. Her love for Ethan, grown urgent and reckless, was a folly that connected only obliquely to the scenario she had devised for winning back Ryan's fidelity and his impassioned need of her. Her complicated feelings for Ethan honed her new self-awareness. These feelings ignited desires that had lain dormant and hidden. Never had she thought she could love any man except her husband, charismatic and impulsive and original Ryan Turner. Never could she imagine that she would blemish her self-image because of her secret infidelity, her carnal revelry, and her sly venturousness. Yet, despite the immensity of her love for her husband, she had fallen in love with Ethan. That her love for him was as wild as it was perverse and rebellious intensified her newly awakened desire. This kind of love challenged and subverted her expectation that Ryan should remain faithful to her. Yet, even as she yearned for Ryan's fidelity, she did not want to relinquish her passionate trysts with Ethan. Imprisoned by her various desires, she was making her way through the dark as she struggled to subdue her compunction and to make a friend of this new, suddenly exciting version of herself.

Excitement lived not only within her newly claimed self and within Ethan's long acquaintance with his rebellious nature. It also lived inside the wiliness and secrecy of their sensual meetings. How long they would consent to this secrecy, they had not yet determined. The impetus of her infidelity lay not merely in her falling in love with Ethan. Nor could the driving force of her betrayal of Ryan fire its powers only through the secrecy of their coupling—hers and Ethan's. That force—that driving power of betrayal—must influence, as well, the startled awareness and suppressed resentment of her husband and of Ethan's wife. Exactly when she and Ethan would reveal their love affair to their married partners had become a subject of debate and had even goaded an unanticipated tension between her impassioned lover and herself. She wanted to maintain their secrecy for at least a few more months and, enclosed as they were inside its protective influence, continue to enjoy the pleasures of their skillfully orchestrated trysts and their unrestrained carnality. Impatient and vengeful, Ethan did not want even those few months to delay the revelation of his affair with her—the wife whose docile fidelity Ryan took for granted. He—Ethan Bromfield Lonergan, at times a loose cannon, a powder keg, a trip wire—wanted to unsettle Ryan's and Ava's belief that they could commit their sensual follies without suffering bruised egos and without forfeiting exclusive rights to the still-young bodies of their married partners.

More than that, more than this declaration of their own rebellious natures and their subversion of society's conservative codes about marital fidelity, Ethan's revealing with her at his side the intensity and excitement of *their* love would surely challenge Ryan's and Ava's belief that they could elude the hurtful consequences of their infidelity and that they could always count on the loyalty of their married partners. Inveterate schemer that he was, Ethan was planning to use his knowledge of Ryan's affair with Ava as additional firepower for his timely advancement as an estimable lawyer representing her father's companies and as a respected member of all the social circles that mattered. He was willing to maintain the secrecy of Ryan's affair with Ava as long as Ryan helped him to rebound from the Wall Street scandal. Though Ryan often treated with contemptuous regard the conservative beliefs that informed the actions of his father and his father-in-law, his well-honed wiliness had taught him that he must maintain in his relations with them the image of an upright and law-abiding gentleman. In all his actions, he must activate the moral codes that declared he was an authentic member of the upper class.

Disappointment and failure had hardened Ethan's character. She respected his wary view of the world and the tough-mindedness that enabled him to prevail over wily adversaries and unlucky incidents.

Cynical and ambitious, Ethan intended to use her father as the agent of his new, swifter climb up the corporate and social ladders. He planned to use Ryan, as well, to reclaim his lost prestige within the social circle to which he by birthright belonged and to restore his relationship with his irate and influential father. The game was about to begin. A few weeks earlier, while explaining to her their advantage in knowing about Ryan's affair with Ava, he compared their situation to playing a game of poker with a royal flush. Perceiving in the information that he had gathered about Ryan and Ava's coupling the analogy to having the best possible poker hand, he (and she with him, as well) held a straight flush to the ace. They had the equivalent ten, jack, queen, king, and ace of hearts. Now he wanted to place his cards on the table so that Ryan could carefully study them. Ryan was a shrewd interpreter of the motives of competitive men and of the scenarios that required him to consent to their machinations. Aware that Ethan held the winning cards, Ryan would need very little prodding to push forward Ethan's bid for admission into his athletic club, into friendships with New York's younger generation of corporate leaders, and into the prestigious circle of the Rhode Island governor and his cadre of influential dealmakers.

So, Ethan kept reminding her while she, fearful of the repercussions that his gambling with Ryan's good will might ignite, kept persuading him that they must wait a while before they showed Ryan the winning cards that Ethan's own wiliness had gathered. Now, on this bright September morning at Saranac Lake in upstate New York, three hundred forty miles away from their Newport homes, Ethan began insisting that he was going to show Ryan the winning cards he held.

"It's not the right time, Ethan," she told him. "It's too early. Telling Ryan too soon will deprive us of many more weeks of being together, free of his interference and of Ava's angry scenes."

Her soft voice and petitioning manner could not conceal her uneasy resentment that he was complicating the scheme that they had been devising together. Through all of these weeks of their mutual seduction, they had consented completely to being enticed by each other and to reveling in their concupiscence—their revitalized acquaintance with their desire and their lust.

Ethan knew her too well to accept this petition as anything more than her fear of losing Ryan's love. There had been other times when she had more persuasively disguised her ambivalence toward Ryan and, despite his frequent betrayals, her dependence upon his acceptance and his love, such as it was. More than her fear of losing Ryan, she did not want to incite Ethan's anger on this afternoon. There had been other days when she prodded his anger as a test of her subtle willfulness and the wayward games that they played with each other. But today, with heartfelt words and a light caress of his arm, she was trying to keep back whatever anger might disturb their relationship. During most of their hours together, her fear of his anger held her words in its chains. Always, the memory of how surly and rough he could be with her subdued any impulse that might impel her to cross him. That she loved him despite this fear—this uncertainty about the brooding man he was—intrigued her. Her love, as far as she comprehended its uses, was a perversity of desire. It pushed its energies against acceptable conventions and against the expectation that this mad desire that held them in its bondage would ever bring them familiar solace or temporary peace. That she preferred the madness of their mutual desire to makeshift solace and expedient peace influenced her now to wait for Ethan to respond to her remark about maintaining the secrecy of their affair.

In this moment, he met her careful understatement with his own subdued response, a disguise that lent credence to his husky, temperate voice and to his nearly affable manner.

"You needn't worry," he said. "I have an instinct for these things. My timing is right. If we wait too long, Ryan and Ava may have lost interest in one another. Besides, I'm looking forward to the pleasures of disarranging their arrogance and of bruising their pride. It's time for their comeuppance. It's exactly the right time to remind them that the world isn't always willing to grant them their wishes. Now is the best time to inform them that, this time at least, the world or fate or maybe just blind chance is allowing you and me to make our own rules. We are answering the call of our own desires."

"But I do worry," she said. "I do worry. If we move too swiftly, we may lose all the pleasures that our secrecy has brought us."

The mid-September sun flowing through the panoramic window touched the lithe form of her. She wondered whether, in this moment, Ethan was looking with approving eyes upon the same young woman whom she had only an hour earlier noticed in her bedroom mirror. That woman who was herself had short blonde finger-curled hair; intense, blue eyes; a smooth, light complexion; a pensive face that, with its turned-up nose and full lips, both Ethan and Ryan had deemed lovely. Did Ethan on this suddenly wayward afternoon regard her breasts as firm and round? Did he think that her hips and legs were perfect? He had often told her so. It was important that he think so now because whatever beauty she possessed must influence their continued rapport and the energizing surprise of their union.

In this instant, though, as she stood before him in her beige tweed jacket and tan jodhpurs and riding boots, he might tell himself that she looked self-doubting and tense. He might wonder whether he was pushing her too hard. He might be imagining that her hesitation could thwart his plans, block his advancement, and ruin his chance to break free of the bad luck that had been hovering, sinister and implacable, around him. So, she guessed and, guessing, noticed once again the tight self-control that continued to influence his response to her hesitation. Before he could respond to her worrisome conjecture, she chose more ominous words that echoed her concern and gave to her hesitation a tough-minded and realistic edge.

"One wrong move," she said, "and we'll lose everything that we have been enjoying together and all the things that we have planned for our future."

Withdrawn now to the mysteries of his stillness, Ethan carefully studied her. Even while confronting his ambivalent stare, she had to admit that his virile handsomeness roused her excited need of his acceptance.

As if he were casting a spell, he stirred her in new ways that never ceased to surprise her. Now, while he drew closer to her, his tall masculinity cast a shadow over her cautious face. He gave her no clear sign of his suppressed anger. Instead, he harnessed his words to the intimacy that he shared with her. At the same time, he pressed his strong, rugged hands upon her shoulders. He was reminding her of where they stood with one another. She knew him well enough to perceive the suggestion of menace.

"Nobody's going to make a wrong move," he said. "Not me. Not you."

She grew very still while she pretended that the press of his ambivalent hands was a show of affection. She could read him very well. He was testing her. If she tried to break free of him, he would tell himself that she was not leveling with him. She was not playing this game the way they had planned. Her breaking away from his hold would incite his suspicion and rouse his anger. Not being able to break away, she would have to admit that the press of his hands upon her shoulders was a warning. The pressure of his large hands and the warning they carried were telling her that he could treat her roughly, if he so chose.

As wily and as manipulative as he, she knew how to respond to him. She brought a smile to her face. She met his gaze directly, her blue eyes gleaming with acceptance of all that he represented even as her intimate study of him concealed her apprehension of the dangerous man he could be and of the complicated perils of their mutual seduction.

Now she chose a spate of words meant to placate his contempt of her hesitation and to allay his distrust—not only of her, but also of anyone else who might prevent him from grabbing hold of the success he craved.

"We'll make all the right moves," she said, after touching his mouth with a delicate kiss. "We are bound to win everything we want. Whatever you want, I want. You will always be in my world now. You are my extraordinary secret. You are my number one man."

Despite her placating words, he pressed his hands more firmly upon her shoulders. Wily and manipulative, he kept his voice low even though it sounded threatening.

"You're not leveling with me," he said.

While his hands pressed down harder upon her shoulders, claiming possession of her, she moved in closer to his dominant physicality. Wary, she leaned her head against his chest. In this way, she hid the look of fear that was touching her face and the spark of pleasure that she derived from the danger.

"Of course, I'm leveling with you," she answered him, all the while maintaining her apparently casual acceptance of his tight hold of her. "I always level with you."

His right hand took hold of the back of her head now as her sun-flecked hair flowed through and across his fingers.

Once again, he brought her face close to his own. He intended to study her as she spoke to him. With penetrating gaze, he wanted to find out whether she was lying to him and whether she was concealing the truth of her feelings even from herself. The low timbres of his voice made his words sound guttural and abrasive.

"You're playing your own games with your husband. You've never stopped loving him. You want him to make love to you again. You want him to love you the way he did in the first year of your marriage."

She willed herself not to move. Within her stillness, she found temporary refuge. No frown furrowed her brow. Nor did her voice rise to protest her fear. Quick-thinking and wary, she waited momentarily as though the stillness in the room that was providing her its refuge was not ready to release her from its safety. Or, rather, she was not ready to be released. Only after that, after this momentary stillness, did she choose matter-of-fact words that might dissuade Ethan from his anger. All this while, without resistance of any kind, she accepted his strong hold upon her.

"Of course, I love Ryan," she said. "I have loved him ever since I first met him. I loved him during our first exciting year together, even when he occasionally drifted apart from me to enjoy some casual affair with a nightclub girl or the latest debutante or Hollywood starlet. I loved him through all the years of his infidelity. I love him now, though not with the schoolgirl love I first offered him. My heart has made room for you. I love both of you with equal fervor, though not for the same reasons. Perhaps, one day soon, when Ryan is no longer my lifeline, I will love you even more than I love him."

Another smile touched her lips now because she wanted to ingratiate herself with him. She wanted to reassure him. She wanted to remind him that she valued his love despite and perhaps because of its furious demands.

Her second smile did not please him. Instead, it increased his distrust of her. During these weeks that had passed so swiftly, they had been playing a game and enjoying all of its fervency and all of its cunning, directed as their fervency and their wiliness was against their unfaithful partners. But in this very instant, the moment after the second smile had touched her lips, she realized that she had made an unwise choice. Her reassuring smile perplexed and angered Ethan. She was playing her version of their game and leaving him at the edge of it. He was outside, peering at her show of happiness and not comprehending it. She might be playing him false, and he had to put a stop to it.

His fury unleashed now, he loosened his grip upon her and, in the same instant, slapped her while he spewed through his teeth a volley of accusations.

"You're playing me for a fool," he said, his caustic voice dangerously low and threatening. "You are using me as a decoy, the lure or bait that will draw Ryan's attention and incite his jealousy. You want his love more than you want mine. But you want mine, too, because it's perverse and volatile and more exciting than Ryan's familiar copulations."

She saw the next slap coming, which would be wilder and more painful. She lifted her hands as if to deflect the whip-like sting of the slap and thereby protect her face, which was already flushed and bruised from his initial assault of her.

"Don't do this," she gasped, as he lurched forward to slap her again. "Don't do this. You're ruining everything that's good between us. Don't play the savage with me, or we'll be finished."

Her words brought a sneer to his face, distorting his handsomeness and giving him the look of a thug.

He slapped her again.

"You like being slapped," he said as he continued to hold her as though she were his prisoner. "Admit it. You like the punishment. It makes you feel less guilty. The slap is your penance for abandoning your fidelity to your errant husband."

He slapped her again, this time even harder. Only then did he release his hold upon her.

She did not whimper, nor did she petition him for mercy or lodge another protest against his brute treatment of her. Instead, she met this latest episode of his anger with the rebellious temperament that had defined her adolescent years. She knew how to tough out a wretched episode like this one. She knew when to call a spade a spade. In this moment, with its electric uncertainty, she summoned from the darkest corners of her uneasy soul the insolence and the defiance that might set her free from the outworn social conventions that had always thwarted her individuality. These new words carried her ambivalent feelings about her adultery and about her insatiable desire to be loved and punished by Ethan.

"Maybe I do like being slapped," she said. "Maybe I want to be punished. That's the price that I'm willing to pay for being a wild spirit. I like playing the rebel some of the time. I like the secret pact that I've made with you, an angry and dangerous rebel who has always been your own worst enemy."

In his anger, Ethan heard her words as a challenge to his dominance. In that challenge, he also heard her conflicted feelings about their assignations—her inordinate desire for his vigorous lovemaking and her anguished contempt for him and for herself.

He grabbed her now and began shaking her violently.

"Enough!" she cried out to him. "Enough! You've had your savage moment. Let go of it!"

She saw his brown eyes flashing with new anger and with the bitterness that was his constant companion, a hoodlum spirit goading his violence. Only when he noticed the blood seeping from the left corner of her mouth did he draw away from her. He held his body taut, as if with hair-trigger energies he was prepared to overcome any new enemy. Still bitter and unrepentant, he hurried to the bar to pour himself a scotch. Here, within the south corner of this spacious reception room and inside the intimacy of their shared aloneness, they had in happier visits to her aunt's grand summer home shared a few drinks and satisfied their intense need for each other. Because her aunt was visiting friends in Australia, she and Ethan had made good use of this Georgian-style house that looked out at the Adirondack Mountains and, nearer than that, upon a blue-green lake that shimmered with the glow of an afternoon sun. The memory of those times intensified her awareness of how much she now needed him. That need still lived, urgent and compelling, within the crafty secrecies that hid her real self, even from those persons who thought they knew her well. These seven weeks with Ethan had with nearly casual dissembling altered her knowledge of herself and redefined her awareness of the tightly controlled unhappiness that was hovering like a sinister shadow at the rim of her marriage to Ryan.

Her perverse love of Ethan was a long and even darker shadow that was overtaking her life. Incautious and self-hating, she reveled in their urgent carnality and their willful smashup of the rules that her privileged community imposed upon its carefully chosen members. Sometimes, she found a neurotic thrill, as well, in her masochistic partnering with this dark-haired, brooding lover whenever he subjected her to pain and humiliation, just as long as he—or perhaps she herself—did not push his anger too far. Her tightly controlled wariness whenever she was in the company of his anger, her undercurrent of fear, and his lacerating doubt of her brought to their relationship a wild uncertainty and a blunt testing of their influence upon each other.

Only after he poured himself a second scotch and quickly swallowed it, allowing its comforting sting to appease his wrath, did he direct his glance toward her. As though his glance contained hypnotic power that drew her to him, she made her way to a bar stool, with its soft grey upholstered seat and its brushed stainless steel adjustable base. Seated there, with a gold cosmetic case she had brought from the pocket of her jacket, she skillfully applied powder and lip gloss to conceal the bruises on her face and on her lips. Even now, she shed no tears, nor did she reveal the fear of him that lived inside her. Instead, with a steady glance and confident voice, she hurried back into this dangerous game they were playing with each other.

"Pour me one, too," she said as he filled his own glass once more. "Straight up."

He was aware that she wanted him to see how tough-hearted she could be. She also wanted to calm him and to assure him that she would always be his ally.

Despite his doubt and resentment, she was well aware that in this very instant, fused as it was with his bitterness and self-hatred, her beauty roused him. Here, at the bar, while the light of the morning sun streaming through the panoramic window caught within its radiance the sinuous movements of her body, her blonde hair glistened, and her blue eyes gleamed. She imagined that, just for a moment, the sheen upon her soft skin and upon her supple body made her look otherworldly. She imagined too that, right after the light of the sun hastened away from her, the room revealed her subtle carnality and her equally subtle dismissal of the dangerous moment through which she had made her defiant journey. When Ethan handed her the scotch, she lifted the glass and saluted him. With a smile that simulated lightheartedness, she offered him the shadow of that defiance as she drew him into her lightheartedness.

"Here's to our love affair," she said. "Here's to making it work for us."

He was not ready to be lighthearted. Her words drew from him, instead, a blunt declaration that hovered about his anger and his despair.

"It *has* to work," he said. "I'm going to go on using your father. I'm going to use your husband, too, and still keep you in my corner while I win other games, as well."

She placed her glass on the counter and moved closer to him, so that she could touch his right hand.

"We are both going to win our games," she said. "We are in all of this together."

He clenched his hand into a fist and lightly tapped her chin.

"Keep remembering that, Tracy," he said. "Then there won't be any trouble between us."

She brought his rough hand to her lips and kissed it.

"There will never be any real trouble between you and me," she said. "There may be a few exciting games and some exhilarating surprises. But we'll always win the games together. That's a promise."

Her conciliatory manner pleased him, even though neither of them really believe that their journey together would bring them any peace. As he answered her, he allowed himself a smile that twisted itself into a nearly imperceptible sneer.

"Maybe we will make our games exciting. Maybe they'll even be a little dangerous. Let's go a few more rounds with this thing. Let's see what happens."

She kissed his hand once again. Then, wily and resourceful, she petitioned him.

"You have to trust me, Ethan," she said. "Our love affair won't work unless you trust me."

He did not answer her. Instead, he withdrew his hand from her caress and silently drank his scotch.

Now she lightened the mood once again and invited him to go horse riding. That they, as a sensual couple, could ride their favorite stallions without being discovered by friends from Newport gave to these Saranac days a special joy and unrestrained pleasures. Ethan reveled in their freedom just as much as she did.

The rules changed for both of them after they met. It was important that they never be seen alone together. For the time being, Ryan had to believe there was no other man in her life. She had made certain that Ryan stayed unaware of her love affair with Ethan. In their home territories in Newport, she had followed the rules strictly, and so had Ethan. Even when they were in each other's presence, they were never together. But here, on this September morning at Saranac Lake, when all of the summer people had returned to their homes in Manhattan or in Greenwich,

Connecticut or in Newport, the risk of Ethan's being seen with her brought to each of them no danger of exposure.

Now, because her reluctance to reveal their love affair to their married partners was inciting his anger, she wanted to dispel his doubt of her. She wanted to convince him that they were still a team.

"We'll have a good time," she said. "You love horse riding as much as I do."

After pondering her remark, Ethan surprised her by accepting the invitation. Though the prospect of riding his favorite stallion did not completely dispel his sullenness, he did bring to his words a carefully measured assent.

"Maybe we will have a good time," he said. "Anyway, swift riding is one way to feel free of all the adversaries pursuing us."

So, they spent that morning riding her aunt's Arabian Bays across the early autumn flare of the land. For that brief time, she felt free. She was a woman who had suddenly escaped from the prison she had made of her life. She was racing out of her own body. She was leaving everything behind her—all the grueling hours and days and years that had battered her spirit and all the good ones that she had eventually betrayed. She was rushing away from even this hour, leaving in its wake the flickering imagery of Ethan sitting tall in the saddle and leaving also, as a spun velocity upon her seeing, the gleaming whiteness of the large main house on her aunt's property. Galloping now, she glimpsed as careening blurs quick verdant slopes and fieldstone retaining walls, ornately paved and planted surfaces, and many tiered, bluestone terraces. She saw as flashes of color and animation young men and women picking apples in a teeming orchard. Paddocks and stables and barns hurled themselves away from her. Houses and farm fields were another flare upon her senses, rising and instantly vanishing. Trees and hills and lake soared, wavered aloft, and disappeared. Even the mountains whirled past her, the pale sun tilted, and the cloud-laden sky darted, loped, and vaulted. She felt freed from all of it. She was someone new. She was claiming a totally different existence. The reality toward which she was hastening was another disguise that might hide who she was from all the people coming into her life and maybe from herself.

Her Arabian Bay was galloping even faster now, at full stretch with body and neck lengthening and each leg fully extended as it powered along the winding trail. Behind her horse's neck, she tucked her upper torso precisely and fused the outline of their forms. She lifted herself out of her saddle, so that she could drop her weight down into her heels and push it further back, allowing her upper body to tuck in behind the horse's neck. Onward and more swiftly she went galloping, riding with shorter stirrups to make it easier to lift her weight out of the saddle.

She kept her lower legs on the girth and kept her arms extended forward, as her horse stretched its neck within each stride.

Other teeming orchards, colorful brush, and wildflower fields went flashing by her. Women and men were harvesting a passing field, and a rugged man was driving a tractor over a northerly hill. Now five or six gray-haired couples canoeing on the distant lake leaped into her vision and just as quickly scattered away. A flight of black-backed gulls overtook fleecy clouds, entered their pockets, and then soared above the white cliff that rose out of the lake. She felt herself soaring, too—rushing out of the reach of the self that she was shedding even as she chased the self that was unknown to her.

Only when she saw in the looming distance two horses grazing in a paddock did she push her lower leg forward while still squeezing both legs against her horse's sides. She braced herself against the stirrup, shortened up her reins, and put the hand that held one of the reins tight into the horse's neck. She used her other hand to keep a strong hold on the second rein, as the horse started to listen and to slow down. The world that she had eluded for half an hour instantly reassembled its imagery for her seeing. Her past hovered by her, ghostly and insistent. The brooding thoughts came back to taunt her. But she fought back. She stayed tough. Her bitterness spurred her resolve.

She wanted to hurry forward to the new, disguised self that she had only begun to devise.

"I'll do all right," she told herself. "So will Ethan. We have made a plan that can win him and me everything we want. Maybe it *is* time to reveal ourselves to Ryan and Ava. Maybe Ethan is right. This may be the best time to take Ryan and Ava by surprise. This time Ethan and I will do everything we need to do, so we can win the game."

Now she dismounted and led her stallion into the paddock that was encircled by a cedar wood fence. After closing the fence, she waited for Ethan. That he would follow her here, she was certain. This secluded spot had always been their private meeting place on all the other afternoons when they had been out riding her aunt's Arab Bays or Tobianos. When he joined her a quarter of an hour later, there was no need to call forth new words that might validate the bond between them. There were no words that could keep at bay his doubts of her or that could disguise the equivocal nature of their collaboration. Instead, they walked side-by-side along the trail that was flanked by lavender fields and scented meadows, accepting the silence between them as a reprieve from his dangerous anger and from her wily submissiveness. Only when this trail left the fields behind and led them to the top of a promontory did she break the stillness between them.

Standing there with him, upon one of the highest hills in the area, Tracy spoke words that revealed more than what his eyes perceived as her simulated elation.

"I love this place," she said, as she looked out upon a blue mist greenery of hills beyond hills, cloud laden implications of mountains, and the sun spotted expanse of corridors of space wheeling freely around and below and above them. "Whenever I come here, I believe in myself more than ever. Maybe, that's because the place gives me the illusion of concealment and a promise of safety. Being here gives me time to rally my forces. It convinces me that one day I will be rid of all my troubles. I will be absolutely free. I will win the game"

This talk of her winning the game once more roused his suspicion. He was, she imagined, convinced that she was playing with him again. She was trying to fool him with her make-believe talk of escape hatches and happy endings. Swiftly now, with husky inflections that yoked themselves to a vague and quiet menace, he reminded her of the way things really stood.

"That won't happen without me, baby. You need me to win the game."

She turned to him with casual seeming attention. Her blue eyes gleamed, and her lips parted in a smile, showing her perfect, white teeth and enhancing her demure consent to his will.

"Of course, I need you," she said. "That is why you are here."

Her gaze turned back to the colorful panorama that apparently solaced her. He, in turn, studying her every move, saw what, with clarified awareness, she was observing. Below them, a motorboat was speeding across the lake, leaving in its wake the spume and ripples of blue-green waters. In the faraway distance, at the edge of the sun-tinted forest that stood across from the lake, Chilean willow trees, Scotch elms, and blueberry ash trees were bringing flares of excited color to the autumn morning. Higher than that, though still within the opaque blue furling of distance, a stray herring gull was curving the dark flash of its wings against the tumescence of ponderous clouds. After an instant's pause, it plummeted with wily skill to the consenting lips of lake waters, the better to pluck for its meal a raw, ample fish or a tiny, mackerel-tinted seabird.

Though the vision gave her back what she had not sought, a predatory image shown natural and insistent, she grasped comfortably its familiar message and found again her realistic measure for understanding things. Turning once more, still toward the east, she was not surprised to sight the zinc-white hang of a wind-bleached cliff glaring like the bones of a devoured world. The limestone solidity of the gargantuan form impressed her, as did the cliff's having endured a wilderness of centuries. The imagery put her in mind of her own resilience, as willful and time trapped as that was. In a world of uncertainty and violence, her capacity to withstand brute adversaries and wrenching betrayals was, she felt, her most essential weapon. The stark message she took from the cliff quickened her senses more acutely than any of the colors of the earth that surrounded her.

She noticed, too, across and above the disquieted lake and on the crest of sun glanced fertile hills—right there, at the wavering margins of the shadow-laden woods—a gray-blue immensity of swaying larches that apparently grew into the sky and, before her troubled eyes, joined all of heaven's restless and eerie motion. The sudden wind was billowing now, like a flare of wings lifted by lower winds and pushing upward against moist, lake-scented air. This feeling of space actively stirring, this sense that here on a sun-hued promontory the wind had come sweeping through the day's intricate layers and, spinning always its rapid coils, had come to claim her—it was this feeling that stopped her firm gait and held her in taut surprise back upon her heels while cliff and clouds and festive autumn colors went wheeling by her. The earth itself seemed to revolve with visible motion. She noticed once more the receding diagonals of the forest across the lake—a shadow flecked welling of foliage and trees, an instant's ambiguity of surface and space. She noticed, too, Ethan's scrutiny of that same sequestered place. She wondered whether in this moment he was maintaining his realistic sense of things. In so many ways, he was just as knowing as she about the world's equivocal promises, just as canny about its bruising, addictive textures.

She turned to him now, eyeing him steadily, as though she were coming back to him after a long absence. His intense brown gaze and suntanned radiance, partially concealed by the light that shimmered around him, gave him the spectral look of a mirage or an apparition. Then, because the whorls of slanted light began slowly to recede from him, she saw more clearly his enigmatic face and heard, with muted skepticism, his matter-of-fact appraisal of their surroundings.

"I've taken from this place what I need," he said. "It has served me well. Maybe it has done the same for you."

"Maybe."

She laughed lightly, giving herself completely to the pleasure of this moment.

"Oh, Ethan, it is wonderful to be happy here with you. Let's promise always to be happy together."

Her blue eyes were misty with tears as she touched his lips with a delicate kiss.

"That's an easy promise to make," he answered her, his words as direct as they were even-tempered. "I'm all for that. Just be certain you do your part to make us happy."

"You know I will," she said, her voice still touched with exhilaration. "I'll always do everything to make us happy."

He observed her quietly, but only for an instant. She saw that he was not ready to share her exhilaration. His ingrained cynicism required here-and-now proof of the happiness they were seeking. That happiness, spawned from their betrayal of faithless Ryan and Ava, would cost them their souls. She imagined the questions that inflamed his brooding. Had she allowed herself to forget their betrayal of the partners that they believed they still loved? Or, in the most secret recesses of her heart, was she more treacherous than he was? Was her contempt of people more furious than his? Was her despair more deeply rooted? She wondered whether these questions were even now scalding his senses. To allay her unease, she persuaded herself to press her lips against his lips and, afterwards, found words that might please him.

"You are so right," she said. "Now is the time to show our hand. Now is the right time to set new rules for our relations with Ryan and Ava."

"Sure, I'm right," he said. "You understand that because you're my woman. You are going to make me very happy."

"Let's ride back together," she said, apparently satisfied that this hour had dispelled his brooding at least a little. "We'll change our clothes and then go on to Burlington for lunch. You can drive the Bentley you like so much."

"I do like the Bentley," he answered her. "And I am ready for lunch."

They walked back to the paddock and deftly mounted their horses. They cantered along the trail in unison. Though they spoke no words to each other, she imparted through her gleaming smile the lighter spirit she had permitted to attend her from the moment they reached the promontory. He, too, consented to a modulated variation of this lightheartedness. During their brief stop at her aunt's home and all through the drive to Burlington, Vermont, and even during their lunch at a fashionable lakeside restaurant, he joined her in good-humored talk of the new happiness they would know after they revealed their subversive plan to Ava and Ryan. There would be exciting weeks in Hawaii, occasional trips to the Bahamas, weekends of skiing in Vermont, and their frequent co-piloting of a Piper Cherokee. But there would be new happiness now, as well. Seductive and serene, she kept whispering romantic words, promising him in the hour or two they spent in Burlington that, when they returned to her aunt's home, she would bring him into her bed. They would see the colored lights again, as they had when they first made love together.

Her lightheartedness, a pre-moral complicity, temporized but could not dispel her distrust of him. With him, she would always be on her guard. That was the best way to handle him. That was how she was going to win this game they were devising every time they were with each other and all the time they were not.

To make their plan work, she had to stay in it with Ethan all the way. Her continued need of him was essential to his remaining in the game and to their gathering the rewards of this game they were playing. On most days, she preferred Ethan's harder edge. She knew where she stood with him when he was being himself, the tough-minded realist who disdained conventional sentiment and fairy tale unions. Each of them had traveled far away from the safe paths of convention and fairy tales. Though she was reluctant to tell him all the disappointments of her past, he had drawn from her enough of the story to understand that Ryan had made a mess of his life with her. But their being the offspring of wealthy parents protected them. The privileged families that had spawned them and the wealthy circles they inhabited continued to receive them as a happily married couple.

Neither she nor Ethan intended to scandalize Ryan and Ava. They wanted, instead, to avenge themselves in more private ways. For her part, she had begun to enjoy the thrill and peril of having taken as her lover a troubled and dangerous man. She was enjoying even more the thrill of avenging herself against her husband, the much-adulated Ryan Turner, who was unfaithful, self-centered, and—at the young age of twenty-five—cynical and world-weary.

Let the game proceed, she told herself, and let the chips fall where they must.

2

Three days later, after she drove back to Newport a day earlier than the one that Ethan chose for his return, Tracy arranged the meeting in which they planned to reveal their ongoing love affair to their married partners. A dinner at their exclusive social club that celebrated Ryan's and Ava's return from Europe would render the confession of Ethan's and her adultery as unexpected as it was astonishing. With its beautiful antiques, burnished mahogany, rich fabrics, and dignified ambiance, as well as original canvases by Mary Cassatt, Winslow Homer, and Thomas Hart Benton, the club provided a setting that was both elegant and solacing. To intensify the surprise that would eclipse that solace, she reserved a dining room on the second floor, where their preferred placement would for the first hour of their being together as two apparently convivial couples enhance the pleasures of the evening. Only afterwards, after she and Ethan revealed the various ecstasies of their love affair and revealed, as well, their awareness of Ryan and Ava's rebellious copulations, only then would the club's refined atmosphere, the upright conduct of guests young and older (that, upon their arrival, they had glimpsed in neighboring rooms), and the disciplined cordiality of the servers enable them to respond to each other with quickened dialogue that restrained its dismay and its vehemence.

On the evening that the dinner party was about to unfold, her intuition warned her that the game she and Ethan had—with malevolent calculation—devised might surprise and unsettle not only Ryan and Ava, but also Ethan and herself.

So be it, she told herself. What must be, will be.

Located five miles from Ryan's and her Georgian-style home that overlooked a lake, the Newport Country Club, with its upscale membership and exclusionary airs, often provided a solacing atmosphere for the dinner parties and other celebrations that Ryan and she hosted. Their parents were members of long and honorable standing here. For more than a decade and sometimes from his

Sutton Place residence fifty miles away, her father has brought his crafty and ambitious drive to his place on the board of directors. Reined in though he was by the conservative rules of the club, he managed to push forward all the changes that gave the club a modern ambience even while he protected the high standards that maintained the club's inherent excellence and award-winning reputation.

To tease Ryan's more-than-ordinary interest in the evening that was about to unfold, she made a casual-seeming remark during their drive to the country club.

"This is an evening that is going to surprise us," she told him.

With his eyes attending the dark road ahead of them and with merely a vague interest in her words, Ryan tossed her a casual question.

"Why do you think so?"

"It's just a feeling I have," she said. "Call it a woman's intuition."

Whether Ryan detected the excited breathlessness in her voice, she had no way of knowing. What she did perceive was his momentary interest that hovered at the cusp of his jaded indifference.

"Well, then," he said, "let's hurry forward to this mysterious surprise."

She laughed a lighthearted laugh as a way of easing the tension that had come there to watch her, an ambivalent Spirit observing her every move.

"Yes," she agreed. "Mysteries can spark a party."

They arrived at the country club in a timely manner. They made an impressive arrival in Ryan's Mercedes Benz, a birthday gift from his parents. The valet, an aged and dignified man with a mane of thick white hair and a face that wore his cragged features with humble assurance, courteously greeted them. His rheumy, brown eyes lighted up with muted recognition of them, but he carefully abstained from any words that might reveal his pleasure in their arriving here on this crisp and unusually cool evening in the third week of September. Rather, it was she who crossed that invisible and sometimes uncomfortable barrier called protocol and, with quietly calibrated decorum, offered him a greeting that was both friendly and natural.

"It's good to see you, Mr. Johnson," she told him. "I hope the evening finds you well."

He beamed with appreciation and quietly answered her.

"It does, indeed, Mrs. Turner. It does, indeed. Thank you for asking."

She and Ryan made their way into the club with a nearly lighthearted anticipation of the rewards and the mysteries that the evening might dispense to them. Two women, pretty with titian hair, hazel eyes, and hour-glass figures and in their twenties, welcomed them with proficient courtesies and helped them to remove their coats—Ryan's beige cashmere topcoat with its oversized notched collar and double-breasted button front and her azure blue sheath coat, with its shirt collar, long sleeves, and cobalt blue piping.

Right after that, a *maître d'* warmly received them and guided them up the long, wine-colored carpeted staircase to a dining room on the second floor, where the preferred placement was sure to enhance the privacy and the surprises of the evening. Before they entered its guarded serenity, they moved with familiar ease through other capacious rooms, noticing without acknowledging them Ryan's business acquaintances and many of their Newport friends that had remained steadfast advocates despite rumors of Ryan's various infidelities. In the southwest corner of one of these room, a young, sandy-haired pianist, sitting with relaxed poise at a satin walnut Steinway, played the romantic melodies of George Gershwin, Jerome Kern, and Franz Lehar. As she had done in so many previous visits here, Tracy scanned the room's well-ordered design with attentive admiration and with a tinge of nostalgia, recalling as she did the evenings when Ryan escorted her here and had eyes for no other woman but her. After the *maître d'* guided them into the spacious room that was reserved for their dinner party, she noticed once again the room's beautiful antiques, burnished mahogany, rich fabrics, and dignified atmosphere, as well as original canvases by Grandma Moses, Andrew Wyeth, and Thomas Hart Benton. With approving eyes, she saw that the room created a setting that was both elegant and stately.

As this dining room and all its amenities unfolded their influences around her, she was pleased that she had chosen so staid a setting for this dinner party because the refined atmosphere, their isolation from the guests young and older who were dining in neighboring rooms, and the disciplined cordiality of the servers might hold her senses still.

She and Ryan arrived at a large, round table that appeared to be waiting for them by the floor-to-ceiling window. The gold-hued velvet drapes were drawn so that the light of the moon that gleamed upon the wide expanse of green lawn fanning out to the even more expansive greenery of a golf course also caressed the more private area where they were being seated. Moonlight touched, as well, the gold tablecloth with its delicately woven jacquard poinsettia design and the yellow, red, and white roses that were tucked into a crystal vase with ivy and ferns. She noticed at once Ethan and Ava, subdued yet sociable as they conversed with each other. She knew them well enough to detect the tension that lived nearly concealed between them. In this instant, as on many recent occasions, she found it ironical that their adultery had brought Ethan into her life in a new and rebellious way. Unexpectedly, Ethan was rescuing her from the humiliation of Ryan's betrayal. He was also wakening her to her wild and destructive self.

Here, in this moment, she was careful to offer Ethan nothing more than an acceptable cordiality. She exchanged greetings just as cordial with devious Ava.

Attentive though she was to the conversation, she focused at the same time upon what everyone was wearing. It was a way to hold her senses still, so keen was her anticipation of the surprise that this evening was going to reveal. That surprise was going to influence the lives of four persons who continued to enjoy the exclusionary privileges accorded to the wealthy and the powerful. The evening's revelations that she and Ethan planned to impart to Ryan and to Ava would give to their dinner party the impetus of disguise and betrayal.

The four of them made a well-groomed party. Ethan looked casually impressive in his gray suit, its slim, masculine lines made perfect because of the symmetry of its notch lapels, waist flap pockets, and dual back vents. His necktie in blue silk twill that matched the blue of his shirt was printed with a red polka dot pattern and a background of blue, red, and gray swirls. Ryan's ingrained charisma enhanced a double-breasted navy-blue suit, with its notch collar, double-breasted button front, and chest welt and front welt pockets. His tie, navy with light blue rhombi designs, nicely complemented the suit and brought color to the whiteness of his shirt. The well-groomed appearance of these men quickened her appreciation of fabrics and colors and their designers.

She and Ava looked equally impressive. Ava's tall, slender figure matched the beauty and elegance of her white sheath turtleneck evening dress. She herself was wearing with understated authority a boat-neck, dark blue A-line party dress that had long sleeves and a floral embroidered skirt. She told herself that she was in her glamour mode. She wanted this evening to work for her. She wanted Ryan to fall in love with her again, though why his loving her was still important she could not say, so uneasy and disarranged were her feelings on this strange-seeming evening when she was anticipating a new turn on the dark path that, with Ethan, she was traveling. Secretly tense and excited, she was waiting for a different rescuer than the man that she kept telling herself she still loved, despite his having traveled far away into a secret world she could not enter.

As soon as the *maître d'* guided Ryan and her to their table and after they exchanged warm greetings with Ethan and Ava, a young, red-haired waiter—tall, lean, and immaculately groomed in a black tuxedo—brought them drinks. Ryan and Ethan enjoyed scotch on the rocks. She and Ava found pleasure in delicate stem glasses of *Veuve Clicquot*.

Convivial within the boundaries of decorum, they began talking about many things. They were, she perceived, playing a serious game. They were sharing stories that included all of them alone and together and that made the memory of each of them palpable and real—invisible and nebulous presences in the telling that came vividly alive and influential there at the dinner table.

Ryan reminisced about their river rafting adventure on the Kitka River in Finland. During those daredevil hours two years earlier, they—as well as her sister Linda and Linda's husband Steven Bradford and a professional skipper—paddled through the heave and swirl of seven white water rapids along an eight-mile route.

"Our hearts were beating faster that day," Ryan said. "What an adrenalin rush that trip was!"

His face beamed with the happy memory.

She had a different kind of recollection. She remembered the adventure with a tinge of nostalgia.

"We were there with two persons who have always been kind to us," she said. "That's what made the river rafting special."

"It *was* special," Ryan said. "Steven and Linda made it very special. Navigating those white waters, they were agile, skillful, fearless, and adventurous. In my book, they are A+!"

She smiled when she heard Ryan's remarks. She admired Linda and Steven because they were good parents and because they genuinely loved their two sons. With Linda and Steven, what you saw was what you got. Honest in their words and in their responses, sensitive to other people's feelings, and helpful whenever they could be, they inspired everyone's trust and respect. Years earlier, when she was doing everything wrong in her adolescence—even then, when her life seemed to be falling apart, smashed up and apparently beyond repair, Linda and Steven stood by her. They reminded her adversaries, Newport conservatives and self-righteous busybodies who were condemning her for running away with Ryan, unmarried and unattended, and who wanted her severely punished, that she was capable of doing wonderful things with her life and with Ryan.

With her soft voice and precise diction, Ava shared with them the elation that she felt when she and Ethan, as well as Ryan and she—Tracy Turner, the wife he often betrayed—went scuba diving in the Andaman Sea, within the Beacon Reef of Thailand. They had traveled there with Ryan's parents. But on that memorable day, Ethan, Ava, Ryan, and she went scuba diving without Ryan's parents.

"I never imagined that scuba diving could be so astonishing," Ava said. Her blue eyes sparkled with elation as she called back to her conscious awareness the lift and surprise of that time. "Under water, I saw mountains and coral gardens sparkle like indigo jewels. I saw each of us with masks, snorkels, and fins and head-mounted dive lights flashing red, yellow, and green. We looked otherworldly and supernatural. I saw Ethan next to me and, farther away, Ryan and Tracy swimming as though we were magical creatures of the sea. I felt that I'd been allowed to enter a fairy tale and that I was being turned into a princess."

As a way of deflecting her tension because the memory of a happy occasion with Ryan was leaving her strangely uneasy, she—Ryan's betrayed wife—made a lighthearted remark. She drew Ethan into its orbit.

"If the reef turned Ava into a princess, did it make you a prince?"

Ethan got a kick out of her question. He laughed a hearty laugh and smoothly lobbed a quick-witted retort her way.

"Ava gives the reef too much credit," he said. "She was always a princess. The reef understood that. It simply spruced itself up and invited her into its color and glitter."

She decided to tease Ethan, good-naturedly.

"You haven't answered my question. Did the reef make you a prince?"

For just a moment, Ethan pondered her question. He was an insider, aware of the game she was playing. With a husky energy that anchored itself to the lightheartedness, he carried the banter forward.

"Well, in that reef, batfish, lionfish, and moray eels were swimming around us. They didn't look like princes to me."

"You still haven't answered my question. Did the reef make *you* a prince?"

Ethan paused once again. Then, when he was ready to answer her, his voice became low-key and serious.

"Ava made me a prince," he said. "She made me a prince the first time she kissed me."

Ava smiled and nearly looked demure. But her artifice could not conceal the flush of guilt that suddenly touched her face and just as suddenly vanished.

Ava's response did not surprise her. She understood her very well. She was amoral, self-centered, and ambitious. She was prepared to stay with Ethan only if he succeeded in rising to the top again.

To Ethan's remark about Ava's having made him a prince, she quickly responded, contemptuous though she was of Ava's duplicity.

"What a wonderful thing to say," she heard herself exclaiming. "And how brave of you. You *are* a romantic. These days, that makes you a very special man."

Everyone laughed. Everyone was having a good time—or so it seemed. She was waiting for the moment when she and Ethan revealed their awareness of Ryan's and Ava's betrayal of them. They would then reveal their own betrayal of Ryan and Ava. She was hoping that the revelation of their revenge against their married partners would give Ryan pause. She wanted him to change his life with her for the better. She wanted the boldness of her affair with Ethan to bring Ryan back to her, without any secret paramours in his future. But way back in the hidden corners of her awareness—way, way back within a darkness that she could rarely fathom—a thought lived, furtive and dangerous. If her affair with Ethan did bring Ryan back to her, if Ryan was willing to begin a new, adventurous chapter with her, perhaps she could still maintain her love affair with Ethan.

Faithless and rebellious, the thought at first repelled her. But she did not let go of it.

She was waiting for Ethan to take Ryan and Ava by surprise. She kept imagining their astonishment when they learned that she and Ethan were well aware of their sensual partnership. She imagined, too, their bitter dismay when they discovered that she and Ethan were enjoying a passionate love affair. As she waited, all the while participating in the lively conversation about their travels, their business investments, and the latest political skirmishes in Washington, she became aware of the suppressed tension between Ethan and Ava. Because she was living through her own marital tensions, she persuaded herself that, at the very start of the evening, even before they reached the club in Ethan's Mercedes-Benz, he and Ava had been quarreling. It was not unrealistic to suppose that, with his anger pent up for so long against Ava, Ethan did flare out his impatience with her and, at the same time, spewed forth words that were both menacing and punitive.

"We've gone over this so many times," he might have said to her, firing out the words that were yoked to anger and menace. "This time, listen hard, baby. I don't want to say it again. We are not spending the holidays in Palm Beach."

Not long after she and Ryan arrived at the club, Ava drew her into the powder room while Ryan and Ethan sat at their table, drinking scotch even as they suppressed the animosity that they felt toward one another. Once she and Ava stepped inside the powder room, with no one else there to hear them, Ava began complaining about Ethan's tyranny over her.

"I'm weary of him," she said. "He wants everything his way. If I don't agree with him, he threatens to beat me. Every so often, he slaps me around. Hard. I really don't know why I stay with him."

Devious and subtle, she chose soft words to pacify self-centered Ava who, without exploring her ambivalence, was learning to love and to hate Ethan, though not in equal measure. It was of the utmost importance that Ava and Ethan stayed together. She did not want Ava to thwart the plan that would enable them—she with Ethan and Ava with Ryan—to carry forward their amorous liaisons without incurring the wrath of their parents and the contempt of their conservative class.

So, with words meant to appease her pampered friend's dismay and resentment, she reaffirmed her own makeshift belief in the extraordinary nature of Ethan's love of Ava.

"You love Ethan," she said, seated as she was before the mirror in the powder room at the start of that volatile evening at the club. "That's why you stay with him."

Ava, while applying new gloss to her lips, pondered her remark. At first, she said nothing. Then, as she began combing her hair, she did something quite rare. She expressed her true feelings.

"Maybe I'm afraid of him," she answered her. "Maybe that's why I stay with him."

She coaxed her further. She wanted her to admit her perverse need of Ethan.

"Maybe that's a part of your relationship with him that you like. Maybe you like being slapped around."

Ava frowned. The truth stung at her, a little. She was no stranger to her perversities, no matter how cleverly she often concealed them from her parents and her friends and sometimes from herself.

"Maybe," she said. "Maybe I do like it."

Leaving the powder room, they joined Ethan and Ryan who were seated inside the privacy of the room that had been reserved especially for the four of them. Both men were talking about hockey and enjoying their scotch. With his suave manner and knack for pushing the evening forward, Ryan ordered Champagne cocktails for Olivia and her. Then he drew all of them into a conversation about their Thanksgiving plans. Ryan intended to spend the holiday with her at his family's compound in Acapulco. Her sister Linda would also be there, with her husband Steven and their two sons. Ryan's morally rigid parents and her equally conservative father would be carefully observing them, eager to validate their impressions that all was well with their offspring.

Ava mentioned that she and Ethan might be joining her parents and her brothers in Palm Beach. But Ethan had made other plans that included her as his dutiful wife. He planned to head to Manchester, New Hampshire, where— as the guest of a lawyer who had helped him through his troubling year, he (and Ava, too) were going to enjoy days of swift skiing and snowboarding and evenings of glamorous dances. Hearing his words, Ava fell into silence. At that moment, she did not want to cross swords with her husband. When the time came, perhaps later in this very evening, she would find reasons to reject Ethan's holiday plans.

So, she—Ethan's secret paramour—imagined, understanding the treachery that was in Ava and the danger that was in Ethan.

Suddenly—and quite unexpectedly because she had imagined that she, and not Ava, was going to ignite the first surprise of the evening—tension was in the air. She was not disappointed. Ava, as willful as she was selfish, was already igniting Ethan's fury. She might as well be setting herself on fire. Let her play out her scene. There would be time for Ethan and her—his secret paramour—to scorch the evening with a fire of their own making.

At the dinner table, Ava pretended to be carefree and even effervescent. She and Ava merely picked at their dinner, though Ava had drunk several rounds of Champagne. As it was their habit, the men ate and drank heartily. She had admired the menu and hoped to draw upon it for the many dinners that she hosted later: red and green cabbage salad with apples, filet mignons with artichokes and béarnaise sauce, Pont Neuf potatoes, and almond-filled Basque cake. Two middle-aged waiters, adept and precise, served their every need. In the proximate distance, near a panoramic window that looked out upon the early autumn glow of the streetlights upon the immaculate brownstones, an accomplished pianist played Rachmaninoff's "Vocalise" and love ballads of Franz Lehar, George Gershwin, Jerome Kern, and Sigmund Romberg. On almost any other evening, the romantic lilt of the scene would have dispelled doubts and anxieties and disappointments. But on this evening not even the exquisite music or the gourmet food or the presence of Ryan and her as close friends could deflect Ava's willfulness or suppress Ethan's rising anger.

Ava wouldn't let up. The Champagne had revved up her courage. She kept harping on the same subject. Ethan was her husband. Husbands spent their holidays with their wives. She had every right to expect that he would share the holiday with her in Palm Beach.

"I'm not exactly a wallflower," she said. "Plenty of guys would like to be there in Palm Beach with me."

Ethan swallowed his fourth scotch and quickly rebuffed her.

"Not anymore, they don't," he said. "Those guys know that I can be very rough. They know that I'll be dealing with them if they try to team up with you."

"You don't own me," Ava said, "even if we are married to each other." Her tremulous voice hovered on the cusp of anger and panic. "I'll choose another man to be my husband. I don't need your permission."

Ethan's brooding demeanor, brusque reply, and heavy drinking transformed the cool-headed and charming persona he had studiously cultivated. His steely gaze and barely suppressed grimace were chained to the fury that, with hair-trigger propensities, was poised to overtake him.

"Shut up," he said, still low-key and guttural. "Stop being a spoiled bitch."

Ryan changed the subject. He spoke of planning to buy a Duesenberg at the end of the year. He and Ethan began talking about The Indianapolis 500 and a terrific driver named Peter DePaolo.

Ava wasn't interested in The Indianapolis 500. She took pleasure in goading Ethan further, in spite of her fear of him. She wanted to talk about her Thanksgiving holiday.

"Maybe it's better that you don't come to Palm Beach with me," she said. "My mother has written that plenty of eligible bachelors will be there—men on their way to the top who haven't got themselves into trouble with the law. She sent me a cable, urging me to change my plans and head to Palm Beach for Thanksgiving."

Ethan's entire body grew taut. Stillness, ominous and menacing, was taking hold of him.

Heedless of the consequences, Ava went on goading him.

"Until Mother mentioned them, I hadn't realized how much I've been missing all the men who can bring me to the top with them."

As soon as she uttered those words, Ethan grabbed hold of her and, pinioning her to his brute force, began slapping her over and over.

"Don't ever mention them again," he snarled. "Don't even think about them."

Ava began screaming. It was an adolescent girl's scream, helpless and whimpering. Caught inside that scream was an insolent warning.

"I'll tell your father! I'll tell him everything!"

Ethan slapped her again, this time so hard that she fell out of her chair. Seated next to her, she saw a half-filled wine glass spill across the carpet and shatter, leaving a stain that looked like blood. The clasp of Ava's necklace broke, the delicate symmetry of its sunflower design still intact as the necklace also fell upon the carpet.

The two waiters—tall, silver-haired, and solicitous—hurried toward their table only to be pushed back by the commotion. The pianist—accomplished, youthful, and good-looking—went on playing the romantic melodies of Franz Lehar, Jerome Kern, Sigmund Romberg, and George Gershwin. Three senior couples passing along the corridor outside their room peered at the confusion with startled and apprehensive countenances.

All this while, Ryan had risen from his chair and was struggling to restrain Ethan. As swift as he was powerful, he passed his hand under Ethan's arm and locked it on his neck. With his other hand, he held down Ethan's wrist while he pulled him away from Ava. For a moment, Ethan struggled against his opponent. But, when he saw wailing Ava hurrying away to the powder room, he relaxed his body. Her hair and clothes were disheveled. Her face was bruised, and her lips were bleeding. He noticed, perhaps for the first time, that Ryan, the wealthy scion whom he planned to use to regain his place at the top, was the man who had drawn him away from Ava.

"Calm down," she whispered to Ethan. "You've got too much to lose if you make the wrong move."

"I had to stop you," Ryan explained, secretly pleased that he had overpowered Ethan, toward whom he harbored ambivalent and even adversarial feelings. "You were really roughing her up."

"I know what I'm doing," he said. "I want her to remember that I don't like being played with."

"She knows that," Ryan said. "Tonight, she made a mistake. She went too far."

"After tonight, she'd better not make mistakes."

She—Ava's apparently loyal friend—had secretly enjoyed watching Ethan beat her rival for Ryan's love. She had made no attempt to stop the assault. Ava deserved the beating. For her, it served as a reality check. Neither the world, nor Ethan Lonergan existed to accommodate all her demands.

With that thought in mind, she hurried to the powder room to help Ava repair her face and her cocktail dress. Ava was sitting before the large mirror that compassed the entire wall. Thelma Brady, the powder room attendant who was a middle-aged woman with a good-natured disposition and motherly concern, was standing beside her. She had already helped her comb her hair and readjust her diamond necklace.

"She'll be all right," Thelma said. "She's just shaken up a bit."

Intuitive as well as experienced, she quickly left the room. She understood that they wanted to talk privately.

No sooner had she left than Ava blurted out her confession.

"It was my fault," she sobbed. "I said mean things to make Ethan angry."

"I'm certain that Ethan feels as sorry as you do."

"I don't know why I said all those terrible things. I really love him."

Understated and devious as well, she carefully nudged Ava once again to do and say the things that would draw her closer to Ethan and far away from Ryan.

"Of course, you love him. But Ethan may stop believing that you do, if you keep on mentioning other men."

"I won't mention them ever again," she said. "That's a promise."

"That's a good promise. Now dry your tears. You want to look your best for Ethan."

Ava brightened. The prospect of using her beauty to keep Ethan at her side appealed to her. It made plausible the certainty that Ethan would always want to be her bed partner.

While they were finding their way back to the dining room, she noticed that Ava was moving with her usual feminine grace and with inherent poise. But, once they arrived at their table, she began trembling almost imperceptibly. Ethan and Ryan were talking quietly about football. Ryan had been able to calm Ethan at the same time that he ordered him to stop giving Ava a hard time.

Apparently, Ava liked being roughed up. In spite of her tremulous air, her bruises didn't prevent her from taking her place next to Ethan and planting kisses upon his lips and neck and right ear, all the while asking for his forgiveness.

"I'm so sorry," she said, as her eyes misted with tears again and her voice invoked a soft sobbing. "You have to forgive me. I love you too much not to be forgiven."

For a moment, Ethan carefully observed her. He liked the tearful eyes and the sobbing voice. They seemed deferential and nearly genuine. He accepted the kisses, though they did not persuade him that Ava's sorrow would be long lasting. Nor did her kisses dispel his ambivalent manner and the equivocating words that suggested his compunction would be as superficial as her own.

"I'm sorry, too, baby," he said. "I'm just as sorry as you are."

Ryan, who became very still when he saw Ava kissing Ethan, did not notice the ambivalence. But she did—she, Tracy Maguire Turner, whom Ava had accepted as a friend to be trusted.

She was not surprised that Ethan and Ava could so smoothly patch things between them. They had done so before. They might do so again. This wayward evening convinced her that Ethan was not finished with his violence against Ava.

Now, because the moments of physical violence that had shaken the cordiality of the four of them being here together were finished with them at least temporarily, Ethan hurried them into a different kind of violence. He meant to shatter Ryan's and Ava's self-assurance and their belief that Blind Chance or wild luck or the willful Fates would always stand by their sides.

He began with Ryan. His husky voice pitched low and inquiring, he threw out a remark that would draw Ryan, his rival for Ava's finite love, into its cunning and its exposure.

"You like being a romantic hero," he told him. "You like rescuing fair women in distress."

Without skipping a beat and quickly attuned to the currents of Ethan's ambivalence, Ryan answered him with measured calm, ironic implication, and apparent accord.

"Always," he said. "I always rescue beautiful women who have a need of me."

"You have been rescuing my wife for more than a year. That shouldn't surprise me, I suppose. Her appetite for passionate men is boundless."

Though she could hear the lilting chords of the piano and was aware of the white-haired *maître d'* and his assistant who were standing in the distance, waiting for their signal to return to the table—though she noticed, as well, Ava's apprehensive glance at her husband and the push of Ethan's challenging words, she focused her awareness most of all upon Ryan, her errant husband, who received Ethan's remark with steely attention and imperturbable composure. Ryan took a moment to decipher the implications of Ethan's words before he chose a reply that was as curt as it was matter of fact.

"You know," he said. "You know about Ava and me."

"I've known for many months. I can be a patient man when I have a mind to be. I was curious to see how long your interest in Ava was going to last."

"Now you know."

"Not completely. I only know that your interest in her is more than ordinary. You've never spent this much time with your other women."

"Ava isn't like any other woman. She means more to me than any other woman I've known, except Tracy."

"You're a greedy man. You want both of them."

"There's nothing wrong in that. They need me as much as I need them."

Now she came into it—she, the wife that Ryan was betraying.

"What about me?" she asked him. "What if I need another man? What if I need a husband and a lover to make me happy?"

Ryan's body grew taut. Clever and duplicitous, his mind was racing ahead of her words. He was anticipating other words that she might choose to disarrange his trust in her. True to his selfish codes, he chose tightly controlled words to subvert whatever revelation she intended to impose upon this moment.

"I can't imagine you taking a lover—not ever. You take pleasure in reserving all your love for me."

"I did," she agreed. "I did take pleasure in giving all my love to you. But that's all changed. Seven weeks ago, long after I discovered that you were giving some of your love to Ava, I began to give my love to Ethan."

Ava took a moment to interpret the meaning of her declaration. Then, with a defiant laugh and an appreciation of the irony that energized this confession, she clapped her hands in approval.

"You're just like us!" she exclaimed. "You have a wild spirit in you, after all."

She was not surprised that Ava found no displeasure in this news of her affair with Ethan. Ava had never deeply loved any man. But her pensive glance suggested that she needed more than a moment to get used to the idea that required her to alter her appraisal of Ryan's wife, who *had* once loved deeply and faithfully. She—demure and upright Tracy who, except for the wildness of her elopement with Ryan, had always followed the rules imposed upon her by her conservative and watchful class—had now betrayed her married fidelity to Ryan. That indiscretion made her no better than anyone else here. Three of them—wily Ryan, bitter Ethan, and self-absorbed Ava—were restless searchers who had on many occasions strayed from the marriage rules that sought to imprison them.

Now Ryan came into it again. His words were matter of fact and agreeable. They took her by surprise. She was aware, as she took note of the slight crease upon Ethan's brow, that these words surprised him, as well.

"Suddenly, you have become more interesting," Ryan said. "You want more than conventional love. You want to turn romantic desire into an adventure."

Though his words made her uneasy, she held herself steady. Willful and rebellious, she pushed away her apprehension. She dared herself to tell him once again that he was not the only man that she loved.

"Fidelity to one partner is overrated," she said. "I have to be faithful to myself first of all. I no longer care to be shackled to our marriage. Both of us are free to explore other relationships, even while we revise the legal agreement that married us. We can go on loving each other. At the same time, we can give our love to another partner. Choosing other partners is your style. You have made it a convenient lifeline. I am learning to make it my lifeline, too."

To this remark, with its cynical and unorthodox textures, Ryan did not quickly respond. Her words were displacing the sureties of their relationship—the guarantees that kept their bond with each other both valid and successful. Still, he did not permit himself to show his displeasure. When he did speak, he chose words that challenged her willfulness.

"Finding adventure through your romantic desire can be exhilarating. It can be a boost to your ego. It can be an adrenalin rush. It can be thrilling and exciting and breathtaking. It can be all of these things and more than these things. But what kind of love is it? It is not profound. It's superficial. It's a will-o'-the-wisp feeling. It's not real love. Call it by its real name. It is casual promiscuity. It is self-centered gratification without sufficient thought about its effect upon your temporary partner."

"You surprise me," she said, while challenging him further. "Do you really believe what you are saying? You have enjoyed many adventures with temporary partners. What about your effect upon them?"

"My partners know exactly who I am. We make adventures. We play games. We have a good time. We never become prisoners of our desire."

Ava had something to say. Her nearly breathless spate of words suggested an undercurrent of fear as she observed Ethan. She brought to these same words a vague lightheartedness as she also cast a glance at Ryan.

"There's no fun being in love when you become too serious," she said. "Having an affair with Ryan has made me love Ethan even more. I see Ethan's strong points more clearly. I realize that he is Mister Right for me."

All this while, Ethan had studied the three of them with angry eyes and tightened fists. Now he chose curt words to break his silence. He directed them at Ava, even though they were imparting a message to Ryan, whom he intended to use for his advancement. He also directed them to her—Ryan's wife, who had made a pact with him that might become more than temporary.

"Go ahead," he told Ava. "Have your adventure with Ryan. I'm enjoying my adventure with Tracy. But remember this. You will be Mrs. Right only as long as I want you to be."

To this remark, Ava at first said nothing. Perhaps, she noticed the suppressed anger in his words. Only after her moment of stillness did she hurry to say the words that might placate Ethan. Deep down, she did not really believe them, but her fear of Ethan pushed her to say them.

"I'll always want to be Mrs. Right for you," she said. "I wouldn't want it any other way."

Ryan came into it once more. She sensed his tension, harnessed though he had kept it. He directed his words to her, the wife who had adventured away from him. His blue eyes still offered her his ingrained affection. He wanted her to tell him how it was with her. He was wondering whether she was going to stay on the unorthodox path that she had chosen to follow with Ethan. He wanted to be a good sport about it.

"What about you?" he asked her. "Do you still want to be my Mrs. Right?"

She did not answer his question. Instead, she spoke of her relationship with Ethan.

"What I feel for Ethan may be temporary," she said. "Right now, I'm telling myself that I love him. Maybe my passion for him will burn out quickly. Maybe it will hold me in its spell for a long time. Whatever happens, I am in the spell right now. I am giving myself to it completely. I am giving myself to Ethan all the way."

"What about me? Where do I fit in?"

She answered him without hesitation. She was enjoying her willfulness. She was pleased that she had drawn to herself once again the attention and surprise and yearning of Ryan Turner, the husband whose desire for her was suddenly reawakening.

"Let's have our adventures. Let's find out what the Fates have planned for us," she told him.

"Fair enough," he said, just as willful as she was. "We'll make our love life an experiment. Maybe it will continue to be exciting. Maybe it will be exhilarating."

"Maybe it will turn dangerous," Ethan said.

Ava laughed a hollow laugh that sought to conceal her apprehension beneath a nearly wary light-heartedness.

Ethan remained very still, like a seasoned hunter who had sighted his prey or like a brooding man who was planning to use his enemies to his advantage.

3

In the weeks that swiftly passed, the four of them exchanged partners whenever they travelled miles away from the home places that knew them. Often, they travelled together, silently daring each other to recoil before the insolence of their secret upheaval of social codes and their contemptuous rejection of conventional definitions of marital accord. Subversive and restless, they navigated intriguing and always compelling excursions as two happily married couples. Their appearing as married couples—she to Ethan and Ava to Ryan—maintained this false impression to those newly acquainted persons who were unaware of the scenario they had been devising. It was easy to find adventure in this deception. It was just as easy to discover pleasure in their jaded testing of their marriages.

They discovered, as well, days and days of guarded ease in the games that they were playing together. Whether they went parachuting from an airfield in Boston or rode palominos on a horse farm in Camden, Maine or dined in a luxurious hotel on Saranac Lake in upstate New York, whether she and Ethan co-piloted a de Havilland DH.50 at the same time that Ryan and Ava flew a Bellanca C.F., whether the four of them danced in the Skylight Terrace of the Waldorf Astoria in New York or swam in the heated pool of a luxurious resort in Palm Springs—whether they ventured into all of these occasions for the sheer thrill of experiencing life that in these unorthodox moments seemed original and exuberant or for the perverse pleasure of undermining repressive moral strictures that sought to bind them in chains—whether it was all of these things or one of them more than the others that ignited their wily rebellion, she could not say, not even in her soul-searching hours. What she did tell herself was that never had she been unmoored as she now was from the self that for all of the years behind her she had been composing.

In these solitary hours, she also confessed to herself that she could be for Ethan only a temporary sensation to fill his still-young time with pleasure and merely a provisional remedy to allay the bitter melancholy that held him in its chains. That he no longer loved Ava with the fierce passion that had made their relationship intense and thrilling, she felt certain. That he was as unmoored as she from the self that sparked each day with new reasons for happiness, she was equally convinced. To her comprehending eyes, she imagined on more than a few occasions that his tightlipped stillness or the vague traceries of a brooding frown or the flashes of surliness were harbingers of a wild anger that one day he would not suppress. On that fateful day, his anger might inflict harm upon himself or upon those persons he regarded as his adversaries. Now there rose within her comprehension the fear that Ethan might bring harm to Ava or to Ryan or to both of them. The game of infidelity that the four of them were playing could invoke penalties that were irrevocable and violent.

Only in retrospect would she later perceive that her intermittent fears were an accurate preface to the violence that occurred on a sun-glowing afternoon in September, when she with Ryan and Ethan with Ava attended a lavish party that Ryan's business friends were hosting at their palatial waterfront home on Nantucket Island in Massachusetts, off the south coast of Cape Cod. Her sister Linda and her brother-in-law Steven were also there, beaming with their pleasure at seeing her and Ryan, as well as Ethan and Ava. She noticed the handsome ease of the men in their ivory linen suits, azure shirts, and silk floral ties—Ryan's cobalt blue, Steven's palmetto blue, and Ethan's turquoise with navy. She also noticed the meticulous rightness of Linda's light blue chiffon dress and the subdued sensuality of Ava's sun-yellow chiffon dress with its sweetheart neck. Her linen dress in gray and olive with a square neckline and three-quarter sleeves gave her a demure look that for this occasion she deemed appropriate.

On that afternoon of splendor and surprise and sudden violence, an afternoon that would live in their memories for all the years that were left to them, she at first felt no apprehension. Nor, at the start of that afternoon did she apprehend any tension within Ethan or careless insolence within Ava or playful rebellion within Ryan. The afternoon rose before her seeing as a festive occasion that melded joy and merriment and laughter. Their arrival at this grandest of late summer gatherings hurried them into a shared exhilaration with many friends of long standing and a few new ones, too. All too soon, though, within the swift panorama that glimpsed the billowing sails of a pristine schooner on the sun-flecked Nantucket waters in the distance and, nearer than that, caught sight as well of young couples swimming and cavorting in the same blue-green sheen of Nantucket waters or noticed here, inside a comfortably spacious and meticulously appointed reception room, well-groomed summery guests quaffing foamy mugs of beer and sipping stem glasses of sparkling Champagne—all too soon from this festive display of a sumptuous gathering and from her sudden and uneasy awareness, Ryan disappeared from his place beside her, and Ava vanished inside the colorful throng of partying guests.

Her sudden unease because of their absence was leagued with Ethan's bitter awareness that, scheming and willful, Ryan and Ava had eluded his watchful gaze.

"They are not playing our game as it should be played," he said, his husky words an incisive and unyielding whisper.

His anger, suppressed though it was, did not surprise her. The four of them had agreed that, in social gatherings like this one, Ava was to stay partnered with Ethan and Ryan was to stay partnered with her. Each of them could drink and swim and dance with other guests. Ava could dance with Ryan one time, and she could dance with Ethan at the same time. But never should Ava hurry off to some secluded place or a secret meeting with Ryan while the party was ongoing and while their friends and business associates would surely notice their absence. The rule applied to Ethan and her, as well.

She told herself once again that Ethan no longer loved Ava with the fierce passion that first ignited their affair and that burned, vibrant and satisfying, during the first years of their marriage. Perhaps, his desire for her still lived, but without the same power or the inordinate need. Perhaps, only the imprisoning influence lingered. Possibly, the charred remnants of desire remained, like the light of a candle that had burned its way to the socket. Nevertheless, he was not going to tolerate Ava's blatant insolence or her contemptuous dismissal of the rules of the game they were playing—all the secret codes, sly maneuvers, and wily transactions that concealed their rebellious natures and disguised their wayward purposes. Nor would he tolerate Ryan's proprietary handling of Ava. Though he, the disillusioned and world-weary husband no longer wanted her, Ethan did not want any other man to possess her.

So she, Tracy Maguire Turner—Ryan's errant wife—imagined, uneasy because she sensed that Ethan's anger was about to unleash new fury.

Without saying another word, Ethan hurried away from the reception area that wore with so easy an elegance the glamour of a ballroom. Away from the casual artifice and the colorful dazzle of that room, he went in search of Ava and Ryan. She, with a taut stillness that matched his own, followed him.

They hurried onto the tawny sands of the beach. After a few minutes of surveying the busy scene, they—Ethan and she with tense and probing eyes—convinced themselves that Ryan and Ava were not among the excited summer people sailing and waterskiing on these Nantucket waters. Nor were they among the rugged young men who had chosen to swim in the sun-flecked waters with their lovely partners rather than in the heated pool that was located in the south wing of the main house. Now they persuaded themselves that Ryan and Ava had chosen the comforts of the heated pool and the amenities of the pool house, with its mahogany-framed French doors, floral curtains and slipper chairs, candelabra-like chandelier, and easy access to the bluestone loggia that faced the teal waters of the pool.

They hurried to the pool area in the south wing of the house. There, they saw Ryan at once, his long, brawny physique at rest on a lawn chair and his handsome face expressing a casual joy at being there with Ava, who was seated in a lawn chair next to him. He was wearing a black swimsuit—a deep-cut ribbed wool tank top over a snug-fitting pair of shorts sewn in at the waistline. Ava brought her innate sensuality to a royal blue one-piece bathing suit that had a tank top bodice and a low neckline. Nearby, seven couples were either swimming playfully in the pool or sitting around the pool in chaise longues, chatting and drinking draft beer, scotch, and Champagne. Aviator sunglasses concealed the language of Ryan's steady gaze upon Ava. The smooth tan of their skin enhanced their looks and the excitement of their romantic pairing. Exactly at that moment, the pentagon-based tumbler of scotch in Ryan's right hand was catching and reflecting the sunlight streaming through a panoramic window and including him in its glow. Free of care or seeming so, he sat in the chair and offered an intimate smile to Ava while the seven couples went on cavorting in the pool or sitting around it.

While Ethan and Tracy continued to observe their errant spouses, Ryan leaned forward to caress Ava's lips with a kiss. Ethan's entire body became rigid as though its powerful muscularity with hair-trigger capacities was preparing to spring forward. As wily as he was cautious, Ethan studied them with a piercing gaze. In this same, uncertain moment, Tracy studied him. Her witnessing eyes showed her that Ethan was looking upon a scheming man that he regarded as his enemy. With equal disdain and hatred, he was peering at the unfaithful wife who reveled in the adulterous game to which he had perversely consented.

Tracy stood close beside Ethan. Her heart began to beat faster. She was convinced that Ethan was going to make an angry scene.

But in these first tense moments that hurried them forward, Ethan suppressed his anger. Instead, he chose to walk toward Ryan and Ava with an assurance that anchored its powers to good-natured camaraderie. He was careful not to startle them or to disarrange the solace that the party atmosphere had conferred upon them. No one else was there, except the fun-loving couples in the teal blue waters of the pool and at the edge of it. Yet, in Tracy's eyes and, she imagined, in Ethan's eyes, too, the happy couples playing tag in the pool or sitting at its cusp seemed nebulous presences—fourteen beings who were merely shadows within some faraway corner of their perception. To her excited eyes at least, she with Ethan and Ryan with Ava were the only persons there.

Despite her excitement, she stood quietly next to Ethan, as though she were a sentry whose guardian spirit might protect him from the dangerous impulses that held him in their chains. In this same moment, Ethan appeared to her watchfulness as a fearless soldier reconnoitering enemy territory. He kept himself at a discreet distance from the place where Ryan and Ava were sitting. When he began speaking to Ryan, he made his words sound both matter of fact and affable.

"You look like a man who has found the path to happiness," he said. "Maybe you'll show Tracy and me how to get there. We want to be happy, too."

If Ryan was astonished to see them standing a few feet away from him, he gave no evidence of surprise. He was not in the least disconcerted. His steady gaze and understated reply held him to well-honed detachment and casual dismissal of their obvious pursuit of him and of Ava.

"Today, old sport, I'm not the man to show you and Tracy anything," he said. "Maybe tomorrow or next week, but not now. Today, you two are strictly on your own."

"You underestimate yourself. You can do so much for us."

"I do for myself," Ryan fired back at him. "You will have to take what's left afterward."

"You are forgetting the pact we made. You are forgetting, no matter how arrogantly you play our game, that Ava belongs to me."

Now Ava came into it. Like Ryan, she had enjoyed a few drinks. His whiskeys on the rocks and her gin-and-vermouth martinis had pushed inhibition aside. The martinis had allowed Ava to forget her fear of Ethan. She met his frown with lighthearted insolence.

"Maybe I belong to you most of the time," she said. "But today I belong to Ryan. Today I'm leaving you behind."

Ethan quickly pushed her words aside.

"I told you how it is with us. You will never leave me behind. I won't let you. I'll decide when we are finished. On that day, I'll leave you behind."

"I can hardly wait for that day," she answered him, still provoking him with her insolence.

Ryan hurried to say more.

"You don't belong here, old sport. Neither do you, Tracy."

"Stay out of our way," Ava insisted.

Tracy answered her with a low-keyed yet incisive statement.

"You're the one who's in *my* way, and I'm going to push you aside."

Ava fired back a volley of bitter remarks and blunt accusations.

"Ryan loves *me*. From the moment we met, he loved me. Now he always will. Stop making a fool of yourself. You were never the woman he wanted. You're not exciting enough for him. In your heart, you know that. You've come here to make a scene. You want to make trouble. You want to steal our happiness. But you'll never do it. We won't let you."

"Don't be so sure of that. I may surprise you."

Now Ryan came into it again.

"Today, the two of you will have to shove off," he said. "This afternoon belongs to Ava and me. You are not wanted here."

Ava drew nearer him, her body clinging to his rugged physique.

"Let's go for a swim," she said, while finding once more the voice that was both mellow and seductive.

In complete accord and in unison, they rose from the chaises longues. Ryan placed his arm across her waist and began to lead her away. Only then, after he and Ava had gone forward twenty paces, did Ethan turn to deliver an ultimatum.

"I warned you before, Ava. I'm warning you now. I won't let you leave me."

"I'll do as I want," Ava said, willful and rebellious.

Ryan laughed an arrogant laugh.

"Old sport, it looks as though you don't have any say in the matter."

Ethan's rage was churning inside him. But he did not shout or move belligerently toward him. He kept his body inside a taut alertness and his voice low and insistent.

"I won't let you push me aside."

Once again, Ryan laughed his arrogant laugh.

"You're history, Ethan—at least for today. Get used to it."

Having said so, he and Ava turned away, hurried forward a few more paces, and dived into the pool. It was a perfect dive. Ryan's taut muscularity and Ava's seductive figure made them a well-matched couple. Once again, the thought that they did, indeed, belong together goaded her anger. That same thought ignited Ethan's wrath. Fury overtook him. Before her startled witness, his rugged face turned pale and wild. His senses reeled. Afterwards, weeks after the scene played out its madness and its savagery, he was to tell her that in that precarious moment the room, with the teal sheen of its pool, its merry swimmers, its colorful chairs and tables, and its portable bar, suddenly pitched away from him. It swayed apart from ordinary seeing. It tilted and soared and hurled itself away. So, to his disarranged sense, it seemed.

In the next instant, before she could stop him, he took the Colt Cobra revolver from the inside pocket of his linen jacket and ran closer to the pool. He fired a wild shot that drew the attention of Ryan and Ava, as well as of all the other couples in the pool. He did not mean to warn them. So fierce was his rage and so intent was he on killing the two people who had betrayed him that his finger pressed the trigger too quickly.

In that moment, he was to explain afterward, he saw only Ryan and Ava, who paused in their swimming and looked back at him, startled and suddenly apprehensive.

Without giving them time to dive beneath the water or to shout their protest, he shot them again and again.

He fired two bullets into Ryan's body. The first bullet grazed his left temple. The second ripped through his chest and threw him away from Ava. From the impact of the second bullet, blood surged out of his back and spilled into the blue greenness of the water. For a moment, he struggled to stay afloat. Then, losing consciousness, he sank beneath the surface.

The room was all the while spinning when he saw Ryan disappearing beneath the water and as he fired a bullet into Ava, who was screaming now in fear. It was, once again, a wild shot, because the horror of what he was doing kept flashing in and out of his comprehension. The bullet pushed its way through Ava's right arm and sprayed the royal blueness of her swimsuit with the deep redness of blood.

He fired another shot and another and another. The bullets struck Ava's left temple, her right shoulder, and her spleen.

Ava's screaming stopped. Her body fell limp from trauma. She groaned with pain and, like Ryan, sank beneath the bloodstained surface of the pool.

From far away, inside the deepest recesses of his awareness, Ethan began mumbling, as if his words were directed to a ghostly spirit upon whom he had cast a fatal spell.

"I warned both of you, but you wouldn't listen."

Compelled even now by the fury that had driven him to the brink of madness, he stood by the poolside and pointed the barrel of the Colt Cobra revolver next to his heart. He placed his hand on the trigger and was ready to fire the bullet. But something made him pause. Was it his fear of the unknown darkness into which the bullet would hurl him? Was it his unwillingness to fall dead into the same pool where the bodies of his two adversaries were sinking? Whatever it was, the time in which he paused allowed him to think more clearly. He would kill himself, though not with pistol or dagger or poison. He would drown himself in the wind-tossed Nantucket waters where roiling waves would pull his body down into the fathomless deep.

So his shattered mind imagined.

With this new resolve spurring him on, he tossed the pistol into the pool and ran out of the room. Tracy ran behind him. In her hurrying passage, she was vaguely aware of the young men—would-be rescuers all of them— who were diving beneath the waters of the pool to retrieve the bodies of Ryan and Ava. Other swimmers, husky fellows and their demure girlfriends, still stunned or frightened by the shootings, stared warily at Ethan and her as they ran out of the room and made their way to the west side of the property and onto the sands of the beach.

Now, months afterwards, her guilt with pincer aptitudes still cut across her awareness that she had not jumped into the bloodstained waters of the pool to rescue Ryan. Had she, in those first moments after the shooting, already believed that he was dead? Is that why she had made no effort to retrieve his body? In bleak, solitary hours, she kept wondering. She also wondered whether her memory of that terrible hour had held, accurate and knowing, all that had really unfolded there in the pristine pool house. Or was hers a false recollection, an incomplete narrative stream of images that still confused her so many months later?

What she remembered with certainty was that the room kept swirling away from her comprehension. The men who were trying to rescue or at least recover the bodies of Ryan and Ava lurched and sloped and dived inside the haze of her seeing. The young ladies who were swimming, helpless and weeping, out of the blood-tarnished pool, and the two or three braver women who were joining the men in their diving and search efforts belonged to the velocities of a kaleidoscope of images, gone wild and nightmarish. The chairs and cocktail tables and portable bar reeled once again, momentarily recovered themselves, and then swung away from her accurate seeing. The room catapulted and hurled itself away. As she ran from its chaos, she believed that it was following and overtaking her. She cried out her protest. There was no fear in the cry. There was only rage.

"Get away from me! Get away!"

Then, always following Ethan as they fled from the pool house, she saw the room vanish. Or had it exploded? She was not certain. Nor did her uncertainty about what was happening deter her from running behind Ethan toward the beach in the west end of the property. Swiftly, they passed the four couples playing volleyball along the tawny sands of the beach and passed the young man and two women swimming in the sun-blanched waters of the beach. All of them were her friends. Some of them waved to her. The ones who were used to Ethan's and her adventurous spirit accepted as appropriate and even inevitable their superb dives into Nantucket waters while they were fully clothed and their vigorous strokes that were pushing them toward the deeper, wind-roiled waves.

She wanted to save Ethan from drowning himself. She swam until she was exhausted, drained of all energy and nearly depleted of the will to live. The weight of her clothes had made her passage difficult. Yet she had succeeded in swimming against their resistance. She had regretted the heaviness of the clothes. They would force her to tire more quickly. Ethan would, she imagined, try to hasten the moment when he became too tired to go on. In that instant, he would plunge into the dark, fathomless bottom of the Nantucket waters. Water would fill his lungs and burst them apart. The same punishing waters would erase his consciousness and batter his lifeless body as he dropped down and down into the jaws of a murky death.

So she anticipated as she swam with punishing swiftness. She wanted to save him. Resolute and accepting, she now recovered her more accurate seeing. What she saw as she swam across the darkening powers of the water were the white purity and silky sheen of cirrus clouds crossing the gold disk that was the sun. Beneath those clouds, six or seven black-backed, screeching gulls were flying south. Toward the east, green hills rose into a forest and meandered into a community of summer homes. Nearer than that, huge limestone rocks rose up out of the lake as though they were the bones of a discarded species. Nearer still, a cobalt blue catamaran, about forty feet long, was traveling fast and leaving in its wake a spume-fed swirl of waves. Nearest of all, the steadfast powers of the wind-glanced waters were claiming her as their own.

Weary at last, she stopped swimming. The waters battered her more swiftly and began drawing her down into an unremitting darkness, her body already bruised, discolored, and swollen from her rough passage. Her lungs began filling with water. Her head throbbed, as though it were imploding. Before she lost consciousness, she felt her entire body shaking with painful convulsions. The darkness of the waters became even darker. She could not see. She could not hear. But something or someone was grabbing her. Weakened though she was, she struggled to free herself from whatever or whoever was pinioning her, tightly holding her arms so that she could not escape. Whatever creature held her in its grasp was spewing light from its head. But the light merely deepened her blindness. Had she died? Who was this creature that fastened its body to her own? Was it Death? Had she escaped from one prison only to fall into a darker prison for all eternity? She struggled to think clearly. Her torturous passage across the wind-quickened waters had washed away the realistic underpinnings of her perception. Those same waters had washed away her thoughts. She could no longer think. The shock of this assailant that she could not see and against whom she could no longer struggle kicked her out of consciousness.

4

On that Saturday afternoon, she did not die—at least, not visibly. The death of one's soul is, after all, a secret process that is known only to oneself. She did not die, because her brother-in-law Steven had saved her to confront the unhappy aftermath to which she had condemned herself. It was he who had held her fast in a rescuing hold underwater. It was his scuba mask with a headlight attached to its straps that had gleamed a blinding light upon her moments before the shock of his being there and the weight of the surging water and the water filling her lungs had thrown her out of consciousness.

She awoke in a Nantucket hospital. Her father, as well as her sister Linda and her brother-in-law Steven were standing near her bed, their faces held to muted anxiety, melancholic affection, and genuine regret.

"We thought that we'd lost you," Linda said, whispering the words as her way of gently drawing her back to familiar things.

A silver-haired nurse in an immaculate white uniform was standing with her parents, carefully observing her.

"Lucky for you that Steven is a champion swimmer, even underwater," her father said.

"Lucky?" she asked. "Am I lucky?"

"Absolutely," the nurse, whose name was Miss Beauregard, said.

"Something bad happened, didn't it?"

"Don't think about it," Steven said. "What's done can't be undone."

The memory of the shooting was coming back to her. The violent scene was unfolding, vivid and palpable, before her. She saw Ethan at the edge of the swimming pool, firing bullets from his Colt Cobra revolver into Ryan and Ava.

She sprang away from the galaxy of pillows into which she had been leaning. The horror of what he had done cut through her revived awareness. She heard an anguished cry, like that of a wounded animal in a dark forest, rising out of herself and out of the taut stillness that harnessed her senses. No longer completely sedated, she saw once again Ryan's startled expression as Ethan shot him and the outrage that lived on the cusp of his resistance when he fell beneath the water of the pool. She saw as clearly Ava's fear and heard her moaning protest as the bullets entered her body.

"He killed them! He killed them!" she screamed.

All the while that she was screaming her accusation, she tried to get out of the bed. But her body, still enervated by strong medication, held her back. Her father as well as Linda and Steven, disheartened by her trouble-haunted lament and by her utter disarrangement, were telling her words that she could not decipher. She heard only her ghastly shrieking and felt the prick of the needle that Miss Beauregard was pushing into her arm.

She could not recollect with any accuracy the hospital days and nights that immediately followed. Not until two weeks later, after her father had arranged for her to be transferred to a private Newport clinic, did she learn about the aftermath that Ethan's shooting had precipitated. Only then, when Jacob Reutenauer, an eminent psychiatrist with thick, white hair and cragged features, had guided her to a clarifying awareness of what had happened and why Ethan had willed himself to act so violently, did she discover the particular details of Ethan's breakdown and the consequences of his criminal behavior.

Nobody died. Though they were seriously wounded, Ryan and Ava survived. So did Ethan. They looked buoyant and life affirming in photos that were circulated in the leading newspapers and magazines the following December.

Her father and Ryan's parents, as well, kept the scandal of the shooting out of those same newspapers and magazines. They paid off the police and a few lawyers. Ethan's father, now eager to reconcile with his son, rewarded Lars, a Nantucket security guard, for saving Ethan from drowning. They also rewarded other beach employees who were smart enough to keep their mouths shut about everything that happened at Nantucket on that September afternoon.

The forty guests who were there that day, enjoying the merriment, stayed quiet, too. They did not have to be paid for their silence. They knew the rules of their privileged class. It was the same class to which she belonged. True, the shootings made Ethan a renegade. But he was still one like them. Indeed, his father, who had hastened to his estranged son's hospital bed, was thriving more brilliantly than ever during the current surge in the stock market.

Through all of the traumatic months after the shootings and during the uneasy months of her reunion with Ryan, she continued to confer with Dr. Reutenauer. He was working hard to save her. For several weeks, Dr. Reutenauer listened to her recollection of the rebellious months in which she and Ryan had freely consented to love affairs with Ethan and Ava. He listened without harshly judging her and with a matter-of-fact openness that she gradually came to respect. She began to trust him. She started to tell him the truth. Now, as she imparted the conflicted narrative that was her life, she did not hesitate to reveal her secret bitterness because Ryan had betrayed his marriage vows. She also revealed the new cynicism that had leagued her with Ethan as they ignited their plots against both Ryan and Ava. Because of his probing questions, his fatherly manner, and his even-tempered guidance, Dr. Reutenauer helped her to confront her anger and her fears.

"Why is Ryan so essential to your well-being?" he once asked her. "What are the qualities you see in him that make his loving you absolutely life-saving?"

Those were the questions that Dr. Reutenauer called out to her at the end of one of the sessions when even the truth as she perceived it could not clarify her obsession for Ryan.

A few days later, when she resumed this conversation with her psychiatrist, she answered his questions.

"I'm drawn to Ryan because he knows how to contrive an illusion of perfection," she said. "And he is perfect in so many ways. He's the perfect athlete, the perfect businessman, and the perfect physical specimen. He also has a gift for withholding himself from even his close male friends and from the women who are attracted to him."

"You say that his perfection is an illusion. Yet you fell in love with him. What made you fall in love with him?"

"I saw him as a challenge. I wanted to find out how close he was to being perfect."

"Do you think you found out?"

"Maybe. Maybe I know him better than he thinks I do."

"What makes you believe that?"

"He's like me. He's imperfect. He's self-centered. He's devious."

"You say you love him. But you were willing to punish him because he had turned away from you. You were willing to connect your own life with Ethan Lonergan, a man who was a danger to himself and to those closest to him."

"He shot Ryan and Ava because they had already killed him, without a pistol or poison or a dagger. In his own way, Ryan killed me. The Tracy Maguire Turner that lived with him for five years and that loved him unconditionally is dead. Whoever I become now will have to be a different person. The Tracy whom I thought I once knew, the one who died, is a stranger to me in spite of our long acquaintance. The new Tracy will have to learn how to live with herself. She will have to learn how to love Ryan in spite of what has happened."

"Do you think that you can learn how to live with him? Can you learn to be new?"

"I'm not sure. What I am sure of is this: The Tracy Maguire Turner that died chose Ryan Turner because she thought that they completed each other. Both of them turned out to be imperfect. Although *that* Tracy died for him, Ryan is still alive. But even he may not be the same person. Maybe he has died a little. Maybe the shock of the shooting did that for him. Only time will tell whether he is capable of making himself a better man."

"Maybe he will change for the better. Life has a habit of taking us by surprise and changing us."

"Whatever happens, we will have to learn all over again how to live as a married couple. We will have to learn how to be faithful and how to make our marriage an honorable experiment."

With fatherly eyes and quiet demeanor, Doctor Reutenauer carefully studied her. Was it possible that this knowledgeable man could decipher the vague yearnings of her soul? She wondered.

"I admire your spirit," he said. "I hope that you can learn to forgive Ryan. You will never be able to create a new life with him unless you forgive him. Let's see whether the new Tracy can do that."

"I'll try," she said. I'll try to forgive Ryan. I may even learn how to forgive myself. I'll keep trying. That's a promise."

5

A few months after the shooting and after their Newport friends closed ranks to conceal the turmoil of their infidelities—hers with Ethan and Ryan's with Ava—she and Ryan tried to become the happy couple they had been in the first year of their marriage. The romantic partners with whom they had undermined their fidelity were no longer available to them. Ethan was maintaining his distance from her and was also maintaining his jaded perception of the world. Currently, he was dating a series of nightclub girls. This week, he was in Boston with a team of young executives that his father was newly recruiting for global corporate assignments. Ava was living on the West Coast now and was already engaged to a prominent Hollywood film director. In this same week, Ava was attending a New York trunk show, introducing to buyers representing prominent apparel markets across the globe her latest line of relaxed yet luxurious ready-to-wear dresses and suits and elegant, intricately beaded evening gowns. After this show, she would bring her designs to runway-style fashion shows in Palm Beach and in Los Angeles.

She—Tracy Maguire Turner, whose insolent journey with them had traumatized her—had not yet let go of her memory of them—passionate, dangerous Ethan and frivolous, self-centered Ava. She imagined that eventually she would no longer think about Ava. But she was not yet prepared to renounce her memory of Ethan and her perverse need of him. She wondered whether she would ever forget him.

For this new phase in her marriage to Ryan that kept unfolding its surprise and its revelation, she—the problematic and furtively embittered Tracy Maguire Turner—and her sometime husband Ryan would be alone together, though the housekeeping staff and the gardeners would be a part of the scene.

All during this period of moral reformation and marital restoration, she had the sense that Ryan was waiting for something special to happen between them. For many months now he had lived with his new desire for her. The intimacy of his gaze, the sensual touch of his hand upon her arm, and the husky affection within his voice told her as much. There were so many ways that he was trying to show that he loved her now more than he had ever loved her before. There were so many memories that his words sparked into life again about their adventures while hiking on the Larapinta Trail within the Northern Territory of Australia, their river rafting on the Kitka River in Finland, their freefall parachuting from a de Havilland DH.9 onto McCook Field near Dayton, Ohio, and their skiing in the Swiss Alps along the shadows of The Eiger's North Face in the breathtaking Jungfrau Region.

There was so much else that he wanted to say to her.

During the uncertain months just past them that, more often apart than together, they had been willfully navigating, she rarely saw him so buoyant and so certain of himself as he now was inside this unexpected happiness that random chance and their calculated venturousness had granted them. Whether the emotions that were quickening his spirit held him to a momentary silence that seemed like a newly discovered awe of her or whether it was his need to explore with her this exciting revelation of the persons they were becoming for each other, she did not know. She saw only that he was eager to share with her the astonishment of his romantic point of view and to listen to all the thrilling words that she might speak to him.

One afternoon, when they had sauntered into the privacy of their summer garden, they shared a conversation that told her where Ryan stood in his relationship with her. This verbal exchange, with its implicated past and its worrisome traumas, also told her how rugged and even perilous the journey to her own reformation would be. All around them the warm July flourishing of hybrid tea roses and floribundas was a flare of red, lavender, cream-white and pink. A long hedge of potentillas, sun-yellow and orange and red, was another flare upon their senses. Three spotted thrushes, with white eye-rings and orange-brown napes, were trilling fluted notes as they winged their way onto the branches of a golden robinia.

Ryan had drawn her to the blue-rimmed well, where—breeze-stirred and compatible—she stood with him in the afternoon sunlight and watched him return her smile. She meant to encourage his hour of confession. She wanted to receive as the stirrings of his penitence and as the outpourings of an astonished heart all the romantic words that reflected his honest love for her.

"I am in it again," he assured her. "I can tell you that I love you with the intensity that I first loved you. Yet that doesn't tell you enough. The love that I feel for you now goes deeper than that. It is passionate and soul-wakening and lifesaving. It is the primary reason for my existence. It is surprise and joy. It is our taking flight together through all the wonderful adventures that love gives only to honest lovers. Whether my love for you is one of these things more than the others—the passion and soul-wakening and lifesaving, the surprise and joy and taking flight together—

or whether it is all of these things that my love is constantly replenishing, I cannot say. What I do know is this: My love for you has saved me from my former self. By making me someone new, my love has saved me for you."

His happiness and his recreated love for her gave her the clues that she needed. Because he spoke of the new honesty of his love for her, she met his confession with words that she deemed just as authentic and, perhaps, far more abrasive. She could not deny that she had never abandoned her love for him. But her happiness with him now seemed a blemished and intermittent thing. No longer did he alone inspire it.

"I am glad that you have changed," she told him. "I am glad that you have found new reasons to love me. But you have to understand that I have changed, too."

His blue eyes, alert and loving, were carefully studying her. As he waited for her to tell him more, he brought his tall, athletic body closer, standing with taut physicality and watchful intimacy before her.

"I understand," he said. "I understand very well that you have changed. I realize that you have become different in so many important ways. But you are still the Tracy with whom I want to share a whole lifetime of adventures."

Carefree and glowing or seeming so, she chose realistic words now that told him about this new Tracy Maguire

Turner, this modern and subversive woman that she had become within these ten astonishing months.

"I suppose that you should take some of the credit for the changes that have made me a different woman. After all, you have always led an adventurous and even rebellious life. Adventurousness and rebellion have most often been the prerogatives of men. But I wearied of standing in your shadows. For a long time, acceding to the mandates of our privileged class has robbed me of my joy of life. Had you been faithful to me, I could have gladly found some pleasure in fulfilling those mandates. But you have not been faithful. I no longer wanted to stand in the shadows. I wanted to enter an adventure, even if it meant living through it without you."

"You've had your adventure with Ethan. I've had my fling with Ava. What's past is finished. We need to put it behind us."

"Yes," she said, unable to conceal the sorrow in her voice. "We need to do that."

Hearing her words, he caressed her with tenderness and with only a hint of the proprietary claim his touch had formerly made. She felt his strong arms enclosing her and felt, as well, the warm lips that kept kissing her mouth and cheeks and eyelids.

"I love you so much," he said. "You are everything that I could want you to be. I didn't think that there could be any more love in me for you. I thought that you already had all of it. But there is more. I have so much more love for you inside me."

The openness and intensity of his words, drawn from his authentic feelings for her, instantly dispelled her certainty that she could give to their renewed relationship all that he was giving, anchored as his openness and intensity were to new-found conviction and keen-minded honesty. The words that he now offered unsettled her. They called into question her desire to avenge herself in subtle ways against his past offenses—all the serial betrayals that had made a mockery of their marriage, all his broken vows, all his jaded promises.

"I've needed you for such a long time," he said. "I've been so blind. I didn't recognize the happiness that unanticipated chance or one of the happier Fates had granted me. You are what I need most of all. You are the only real happiness I've known."

"Those are handsome words," she said. "If they are true, they might easily cast a spell over a woman."

"They are true," he answered her. "Give me a chance. Give me time. I'll prove that every one of them is true."

"Go right ahead," she said with apparent lightheartedness. "I'll be watching. I'm not going anywhere."

He laughed his husky laugh.

"Fair enough," he said. "We'll make a good time of it."

She was grateful that he did not notice her unease. Instead, he smiled. Her agreeable words were the ones he had expected her so say. But the warm glow of his eyes did not ease her. It intensified her awareness that she could no longer be completely honest with him. His new love of her seemed so authentic that it made her conflicted love of him seem small and synthetic. She imagined that, in the uneasy days that would come as though they were pursuing her, her failure to love him completely would steal her peace and teach her their harsh lessons. Even if she and Ryan restored their relationship, even if she learned to love him once again with tender care and genuine affection, she could envision only a lifetime of unfulfilled dreams and secret longings. Ethan was no longer available to her. Whether she would find a way to bring him back into her life, whether he returned because of his inordinate desire for her, whether the complexities of their mutual desire would influence a renewal of their sensual pact—all these questions and suppositions and dreamlike expectations could not yet yield the answers that she was seeking. Nor could they resolve the dilemma that faced her.

She had not discovered a way to live without Ryan. She had not yet found a way to live without Ethan. Nor had she devised a way to bring Ethan back into her life. Come what may, she must do everything to conceal from Ryan her longing for Ethan.

In the weeks and months that swiftly passed after she had lived out her tryst with Ethan, she could not bear to meet Ryan's inquiring glances or—with charm and self-assurance—to share his warmhearted remarks. During her days and nights with Ethan, something exciting had been given her and something essential had been taken away. Ethan had given her his dangerous love and, by so giving, had released her from the propriety that had too often imprisoned her. The experience had often thrilled her, even as it had satisfied her need to rebel against her errant husband. Her love for Ethan, a bitter and volatile man, had also quickened her contempt for her wrongdoing. All during this period when she was struggling to subdue her own errant will and overcome her self-destructive impulses, she was determined to resist the spell that Ethan's love had cast upon her. She kept insisting to herself that her feelings for Ethan were no more than an unhappy woman's wayward response to an unanticipated love affair.

What she had lost was her fidelity to Ryan. No longer did she feel at ease with him. She loved him still, but without the joy and the purity that in her mind had made of her his devoted partner—a woman who never permitted any man to touch her except her husband. Always before she submitted to Ethan, she had either disdained or pitied the women in her circle who had entered extra-marital affairs. That, until her arrangement with Ethan, she had maintained her fidelity to Ryan had much to do with her having fallen in love with Ryan when she was a girl in her teens. Each of them became the other's obsession. Each of them found in each other the only partner who could be authentic. Though Ryan had slept with other girls before he came to her, she was not disappointed. By the time he was twenty and sleeping with her for the first time, he was an experienced and generous lover. He taught her how to find pleasure in her sensuality and how to make their hours together a passionate experiment.

Now, six years later, she regarded herself as a woman who knew a little more about herself. In this new cycle of her life, she had fallen in love with a man who was not her husband. He was a man who had sometimes given her a rough time. He was also a man who was capable of avenging himself against his enemies in violent ways. The experience troubled her. But it also awakened her to her perverse need of being in his company. Even now, when she was struggling to restore her relationship with Ryan, she kept Ethan in her thoughts. His being a loose cannon, a trip wire, a time fuse only made him more desirable. She wanted "to seize the opportunity." She wanted to be with him. She wanted to carry forward the more complete version of her womanhood that with him she had been realizing. On those days when, with unstinting honesty, she looked within her reprehensible motives, she admitted that her wanting Ethan belonged to a plot by which she might willfully destroy both Ryan and herself. At the same time, because she was aware of how tattered her loyalty to Ryan had become, she was suffering anguish and regret that she had not yet learned how to elude or to accept.

In the weeks that followed their conversation within a secluded garden on their Newport estate, she was careful to engage in the lighthearted repartee that gave special pleasure to Ryan. They laughed while reminiscing about the storm-fed and rebellious sailing adventure that, six years earlier, lived at the cusp of scandal and led to their unanticipated marriage. They shared happy words, as well, when they recalled a water-skiing race with three other couples during a vacation in Palm Beach. They discovered new elation in their memory of white-water rafting on Kennebec River in Maine and trout fishing on Clyde River in Vermont. They relived, too, the exhilaration they had experienced when they attended a New Year's Eve ball within the Ritz Carlton in New York.

She recalled, as well, though in solitary moments without Ryan to share his memory of the occasion, a journey to England that they had made with her sister Linda and her brother-in-law Steven. In the Spring of that year, she had discovered for the first time Ryan's adulterous betrayals. She had told no one—not her sister or her father or Ryan's parents. What good would that have accomplished? Ryan might have withstood the enmity of her father and her sister. He might have forgiven her for having revealed to them his various indiscretions. But he would never have forgiven her for divulging his errant ways to his parents. Nor would he have offered her even his makeshift love that gave to their marriage a polished veneer of ardent fidelity and agreeable reciprocity.

In that Spring nearly two years earlier, shortly after she discovered Ryan's betrayals, she consented to the journey to England as a sensible route that might teach her how to accept the uneasiness of her dilemma. With Ryan, Linda, and Steven, she appeared buoyant and agile as they cycled along the picturesque Monsal Trail in the Derbyshire Peak District. With lighthearted camaraderie (or its credible appearance), she stood at the top of Monsal Head and looked out upon a blue-mist greenery of hills beyond hills, cloud-laden implications of mountains, and the sun-spotted expanse of corridors of space wheeling freely around and below and above them.

On other days when she had harnessed her energies to equally permissible scenarios, she—with Ryan, Linda, and Steven—would hike briskly through the various trails that drew them away from their comfortable hotel into the painterly villages and towns that served them as affable neighbors. One extraordinary time, they climbed the Derwent Edge, which is a Millstone grit escarpment that lies above the Upper Derwent Valley within the Peak District National Park. The guide accompanying them explained that glaciers in the last ice age had scraped away most of the gritstone that had originally covered the Peak District. Raw nature, as predominant here as it was arbitrary, had—through centuries of wind, rain, and frost—formed oddly shaped crags or tors. The one that she noticed, especially, was called The Coach and Horses, because the gritstone that formed it resembled a coach and horses on the horizon. Though she recognized the shape, she was less impressed by the surprise of the imagery than by the stone's having endured a wilderness of centuries.

The imagery put her in mind of her own resilience, as willful and time trapped as that was. In a world of uncertainty, misfortune, and suffering, her capacity to withstand wily adversaries and wrenching betrayals was, she believed, her most essential weapon. The stark message that she took from the stones eased her senses more profoundly than even the rare and colorful beauty of the earth that surrounded her.

She could not, of course, ignore that beauty. Across much of the moorland around Derwent Edge, there lived—vivid and charismatic—the Eurasian golden plover and the red grouse, as well as the kinetic individuality of the ring ouzel and the mountain hare. Species of plants as various as they were rare included common cotton grass, mountain strawberry, and crowberry. In former days, when her happiness was authentic, her sighting such remarkable specimens would have quickened her scientific curiosity and her satisfaction. But in this period, when her awareness of Ryan's adulterous relations was slowly burning away her soul, she could summon merely a modulated enjoyment that was anchored nonetheless to a disguise of her unease while in Ryan's company and in the company of Linda and Steven.

When, after each day's excursion, they returned to the hotel in Derbyshire, she would on some late afternoons linger, solitary and brooding, in a splendid garden. There, with her scientific and unsentimental perceptions, she observed the lavender-blueness of South African plumbago and the dark burgundy and bright green leaves of the Fijian fire plant. But not even their natural splendor could rouse her botanical aptitudes. Nor could the tupelo's canopy of sweeping branches and its graceful flares of orange and red hues content her musing mind that in no new way at all had resolved her festering distrust of Ryan.

Her sister noticed her melancholy. When they were alone in their hotel suite, Linda advised and consoled her. Her sister's blue-eyed, titian-haired presence seemed now, more than ever before, a special radiance.

"I've been aware of how sad you are," she said. "Is there anything that I can do to help you?"

The honesty of her sister's concern for her and the integrity of her well-ordered life moved Tracy in an altogether new way. Years earlier, she had regarded her upright sister as too conservative in the way that she chose to live and too rigid a guardian of the rules set forth by the class into which they had been born. But on this memorable afternoon, Linda revealed a sensitive awareness of the sorrow that was making a prisoner of her younger sister. Her sisterly affection and her genuine helpfulness revealed her sturdy character and her steadfast morality. It was not difficult to open her mind and her heart to Linda, who was so concerned for her well-being.

Quickly, she told her about Ryan's frequent infidelities.

That afternoon in Derbyshire, after hearing about Ryan's ruthless betrayal of his marriage vows, Linda had offered her advice that she would always value.

"We all make mistakes," she said. "Maybe one day Ryan will realize that his mistakes are beginning to punish him. Maybe eventually he will understand that the wrong choices he makes will go on punishing him for a long time. We can hope that one day he will choose to journey along a better path. In the meantime, be patient. Keep honoring your marriage vows. Make your union with Ryan as solacing as it can be. Keep believing that, in spite of his infidelity, he still loves you. Keep giving him reasons to go on loving you."

For many weeks after their conversation, Linda's temperate remarks worked their influence upon her solicitous and loving behavior toward Ryan. But, even while he accorded her both respect and affection, Ryan continued his affair with Ava. Forgetful then of her sister's wise counsel and weary of her docile response to Ryan's infidelity, she initiated her plan for avenging herself against both Ryan and Ava. That she could so willfully abandon her sister's prudent counsel and abandon, as well, her own steadfast regard of Ryan as a man both perfect and exemplary gave her pause. Her reckless violation of her marriage vows and her need to invoke a stern revenge against Ryan made her acquainted with the darker inclinations of her character. No longer could she think of herself as upright and innocent. She had committed a crime against the sanctity of her marriage vows. She had committed a crime against herself.

6

Now, Ryan and she were back in Newport nearly two years after that journey to the Derwent Peak and a year after their experiment in marital infidelity—hers with Ethan and Ryan's with Ava—had nearly destroyed their lives. With her tensile aptitudes for disguise prevailing, she was now trying to recover the fervor of that first year when she fell into love with Ryan and believed that, for all the wonderful days that remained to her, she would always love him. Always, she would regard him as a gift from the Kind Fates or, perhaps, from Joyful Chance that occasionally conferred special blessings and superior gifts upon young women who remained faithful to the man they called husband—the same man whose transgressions they were willing to forgive.

That first year of loving Ryan and loving him for three years after that seemed so far away—a storied past of ardent fidelity and unquestioning belief in his loyalty. No longer did she regard him as the ideal mate or as the only man that she would ever love. Perhaps, she loved Ethan even more—Ethan with his dangerous inclinations and his deep-seated anguish. Her own anguish told her that, because of their mutual suffering, she and Ethan were soulmates. Together or apart, they would always be soulmates. That they might never again see one another deepened her anguish. Always now, she worked hard to conceal her sorrow.

Occasionally, and possibly because he noticed the melancholy that she struggled to suppress, Ryan asked her about Ethan. She always answered every one of his questions with clipped and understated remarks about the wild year that she had lived through with Ethan. Her words made Ryan believe that she regarded her time with Ethan as finished—a will-o'-the wisp attraction that quickly burnt away its light, a foolish dalliance that revealed a fault line in her character, a troubled infatuation that ignited her confusion, a madcap interlude that threw her into a maelstrom of betrayal and violence.

"All that is behind me now," she assured him. "My living outside myself, as though I were an altogether different person, helped me to survive my year with Ethan."

Her words carried a conviction that appeared natural and extemporaneous.

"You are savvy," he said, "and you have a good brain. You know when a risk is worth taking and when it's time to pull away."

His belief in her complicated her remorse. There was purity and idealism in that belief that she could no longer emulate. Now her guilt overtook her with furious powers. She could not bear to meet Ryan's good-natured inquiries or his abiding trust in her ability to reclaim that Tracy Maguire Turner that existed before her conflicted year with Ethan. Though she had apparently rescued herself from Ethan, though with seeming finality she had turned away from Ethan's sullen love, she had broken the bond with her husband that made their love very special, indeed. It did not take Ryan long to notice how she turned away from his glances, whether his discerning eyes were probing her enigmatic face or studying her with his familiar, sensual need. He began noticing, too, how—whenever he caressed her shoulders or touched the soft skin of her arms or held her close to his body so that he could breathe the fragrance of her hair or fondle her ample breasts or lightly kiss her lips—she would stiffen, held taut by what she now received as the surprise of his intimacy, as though he were a stranger.

Once, after she had pulled away from his embrace of her, he drew her back. She had no choice except to turn around and confront his careful regard of her.

"What's the matter?" he asked. "Why are you so tense?"

"Don't worry about me," she said. "I've had a few bad nights. Some of the mistakes I've made during this past year have come back to haunt me."

"Let them go," he said. "Push them back to the past where they belong. Forget all of them."

She laughed a hollow laugh that he seemed to accept as the real thing.

"If only I could," she answered him. "If only I could forget, I would be a much happier woman."

The frown that lightly creased his brow told her that he was concerned about her. He wanted her to be happy. He wanted her to be at peace with herself. She recognized as well the playful wit that quickened his next remark and that brought a grin to his face.

"Don't think about this past year," he said. "Think about something else—or someone. Think about me."

"I will," she said. "I *will* think about you. You will rescue me from all my doubts and fears."

The smile left his face. He considered the implications of her words before calmly imparting new encouragement.

"I want it to be the way it used to be in that first year we were together."

"If only it could be," she said. "If only we could get back everything that we had in that first year."

He pondered the sorrowful undercurrent in her words. He was wondering whether her sorrow was a sign of her helplessness. He had not imagined that she would make herself a victim of the rebellious year to which she had given her wholehearted consent. Intuitive and toughminded, he threw out a lifeline in the event that she needed one.

"Well, then," he said, "let's get on with things. Let's get back what we had in our first year together."

For the rest of that day and for many days afterward, he watched her with keen-minded naturalness. She felt his quiet-seeming glance taking her in. She saw love in his eyes, and she saw uncertainty. The eyes took her in carefully, as though they were observing a young woman whom he had once known so well. In his years of infidelity, he had lost touch with her, with the wife that his wily conduct had made a stranger. She guessed at what the mind behind his eyes was thinking. She was a new version of the Tracy about whom he had once believed he knew everything essential. But she was no longer the same woman. In so many ways, she had become different.

Even when he made love to her now, she was different. No longer was there between them the elated symmetry, the smooth and natural rhythms of their bodies together, their teasing and constant momentum, and the protracted joys of their climaxes. Their intercourse became a shared and ambivalent tension. Whatever pleasures remained were part of a compulsive biological act. Gone was her roused happiness when, naked and erect, he would enter her—vigorous, spermatic, and proficient. Gone, too, was her belief that she was in love with him alone.

Whether Ryan saw that she loved him less than she had once loved him, whether he saw that it was also herself that she could not love or accept, whether he guessed that with him she could never again be authentic—whether it was one of these things or all of these things that might in the end destroy their relationship, she could not with steadying conviction persuade herself. Her inability to give herself completely to Ryan was anchored to the perversity of her having found pleasure with Ethan. Through all those rebellious days and nights with him, through every masochistic hour with him and through every one of their sadistic and maddening encounters, she had accepted their affair as some furious revenge that she was enacting not only against Ryan, but also and predominantly against herself.

To Ryan's searching eyes, her appearance of guilt convicted her. Whatever had changed between them involved Ethan. With each day and night that passed uneasily between them, he grew certain of that.

"There *is* something wrong," he declared. "You need to tell me about it. Never again can there be anything authentic between us if you are going to go on hiding the truth from me."

Of her enigmatic behavior, he reminded her every day. As if they were in a judge's chambers and he, as her husband, was challenging her to defend herself, he began to confront her with incisive questions and a refusal to be satisfied with her equivocating remarks.

One question in particular became the familiar prologue to his interrogations.

"What did you promise Ethan?" he often demanded to know. "What made him allow you to back away from your relationship with him?"

Grown weary of his militant questioning and the angry bluntness of his accusations, she usually answered him in a warm, natural-sounding voice. She wanted to subdue his anger. She wanted him to draw upon the coolheaded detachment that had often been his ally in the years when he was secretly estranged from her. If she maintained her self-assured manner and the poise that suggested she was at ease with herself, he might perhaps accept her words as genuine. Her understated smile was still another expression meant to invoke his belief in all that she was telling him. At the same time, she found pleasure in reminding him of his infidelities. She enjoyed casting a cloud upon his belief that they could once again share a love that was mutually honest and mutually fulfilling.

"I convinced him that Ava's love for him was greater than any feeling I might have for him. I persuaded him that our relationship was merely an interlude, a respite from the disappointment of our marriage, a suspension of dismay at your betrayals, an interval of new-found excitement with him."

She was careful not to mention Ethan by name because that name upon her lips might rouse Ryan's tautly harnessed anger.

Like a commanding officer circling a captured enemy, he would—with penetrating glare—study her quietly as with rugged authority he moved about her. Never, in the beginning, did he raise his voice or alarm her with the driving intensities of his suspicion and of disappointment at her reluctance to find elation in the restoration of their marriage.

"When did you realize that his love for you was a temporary thing?" he demanded to know. "When did you understand that our love was essential for your happiness?"

"After the shooting," she lied to him. "It was then that I knew for certain that he was incapable of loving anybody."

She turned away from Ryan then, tight-lipped and bitter because his infidelity had wrecked her unquestioning belief in him and because Ethan's sadistic love had become an immolation that she invited, an anguish that she craved, a punishment that yoked itself to sexual thrills and self-hatred.

On that occasion, Ryan held himself inside a stillness that presaged a coming storm. The silence pervading the room unsettled her. When she turned to face him once again, he was not there. His sudden disappearance seemed supernatural and ominous.

On more favorable days, when his schedule allowed him free time, he joined her in the activities that held them to their proper course. They rode their favorite Appaloosas along the horse trail and across the undulating hills behind their home. Or she prepared him a favorite meal with the assistance of their cook. Or she worked on the portrait that she was painting of his parents as the ideal couple that she used to believe they were emulating.

The few times that he referred to her affair with Ethan without mentioning his name, she told him that she had forgotten all about those months. Once again, she called the affair a schoolgirl's infatuation, a temporary aberration, a spurious rebellion, an act of desperation.

Nevertheless, he noticed the muted intricacies of her melancholy as she recalled that episode. It was only a matter of time before he confirmed his suspicions that she had not forgotten Ethan at all.

One evening, when he was dressing for a sumptuous celebration that his parents were hosting for their Asian friends, Ryan came upon a diamond ring in a drawer where he expected to find his handkerchiefs. He guessed that Ethan had given the ring to her. She must have placed it hastily beneath the handkerchiefs, convinced that she was concealing it inside the drawer that held her own handkerchiefs. He surmised that his unexpected entrance into their bedroom earlier that day may have compelled her to conceal the ring as quickly as she could. Made uneasy and perhaps apprehensive by his sudden appearance, she had failed to choose the correct drawer. While he was away on business in Hong Kong, she had enjoyed the embrace of the ring about her finger. In the weeks before his return, for all those mornings, afternoons, and evenings, she had savored the impress of its reality upon her skin.

That thought, she soon discovered, maddened Ryan.

A few minutes later, she entered the room adjusting her diamond earrings and reviewing in the long mirror at the side of the Louis XVI armoire the glamorous image she inhabited while wearing a black chiffon evening dress. On this night, she appeared to inhabit, as well, the epitome of self-possession. The recovered serenities of their recent days had disarmed her. She believed that she had won back Ryan's trust or, at least, his patient acceptance.

Momentarily silent and bitter, he glared at her. The grimace that overtook his handsome face stopped her in her tracks. The harshness of his stare reinforced her tense awareness that something was wrong.

Now, opening the palm of his right hand, he showed her the ring that she believed she had concealed from him.

She did not turn pale and tremulous. In the surprise of this confrontation, she revealed no fear of him. Because her guilt rose up to accuse her, she willed herself to accept whatever words he chose to indict her for her transgressions. She wanted him to punish her. At the same time, she wanted to punish him. Observing him as he stood before her with the ring in his hand, she enclosed herself in silence that matched his own. An enigmatic smile poised itself upon her lips. She imagined that Ryan may have seen in that smile a worldly resignation or a hint of philosophy. Perhaps, he saw that she was going to admit the truth of the ring and her willful possession of it. There would be within her responses neither petition nor tears.

Ryan was too personally involved to see beyond her guilt and her defiance. He failed to see that he had often given expensive gifts to his temporary women. Time and time again, he had committed adulterous transgressions not unlike the one that she had shared with Ethan. Nevertheless, with a gesture as stinging as his whiplash rebuke, he stepped closer in front of her and placed the ring in her hand.

"Is this what Ethan paid you after he fucked you?"

She recognized the enmity in his words. They were the weapons that, for this moment, he was using to hurt her.

"I'm glad you found it," she said. "It makes it easier now to give the ring away. I plan to sell it and to donate the money to the Red Cross."

Very carefully, she returned the ring to her jewelry box and, with self-assured and nearly balletic movements, placed the box inside a private drawer in her dresser.

By maintaining her calm, she might draw him away from his resentment and his jealousy. But his rising anger made her aware that he would not let go of his desire to punish her. He could not forgive her for destroying his belief that they could recapture the honest joys of their first year together.

"You haven't answered my question," he said, as he followed her to the dresser. He might have been a hovering nemesis or an implacable Spirit planning to punish her. "You haven't told me why you saved that ring."

She had kept her back to him, even after she had returned the ring to its proper drawer. Her refusal to admit Ethan's continuing hold upon her compelled her to hide her face from him. He was aware of a new hardness in her parrying his remarks. That, along with the clear-headed decorum she quietly imparted as though it were the armature protecting her, roused his anger to a new level. Now he grabbed her roughly and brought her face to face with him.

"Tell me the whole thing," he demanded. "Tell me why you were saving that ring."

She remained very calm. Enclosed within her momentary stillness, she allowed herself the hint of a smile. Perhaps, her smile and her calm might persuade him that the ring had no real importance to her. Both the calm and the smile came from a hardened place in her heart.

"I saved the ring because of its value," she said. "I've already told you that I intend to sell the ring to a jeweler and donate the money from the transaction to the Red Cross."

Ryan refused to believe her.

His anger coiling itself about his sullen regard of her, he would not accept her words. She saw that, despite the conviction she brought to those words, Ryan found them contrived as well as clever.

"You saved that ring because you and Ethan are not finished. You are waiting for him to contact you. The two of you have a few more adventures ahead of you. Tell me that, and I'll believe you."

He kept his deep voice low and insistent as he snarled his words out to her. Although their brooding timbres held themselves at the cusp of understatement, his words sounded threatening.

She was weary of him. His doubts and his accusations had made him mean-spirited and tiresome. There was, she had to admit, some pleasure in unsettling his belief in her as his faithful wife and in her promise to be once more and forever afterward the Tracy Maguire Turner she used to be when they first met and for the magical first four years of their marriage. She found pleasure, too, in his emerging awareness that she was not that Tracy, nor could she be that Tracy ever again.

If Ryan was not yet prepared to accept the Tracy that she now was, she could not accept this brooding version of him. Always, before this year after the shooting, Ryan's realism had been his ballast against confusion. A shrewd detachment and a cosmopolitan sensibility had quickened his perception. Because of them, he had avoided emotional displays as well as inaccurate readings of the reality unfolding around him. She preferred *that* Ryan Turner. This adversary standing here before her, with his suppressed anger and his muted jealousy, was some other Ryan—an inauthentic variant, a doubting and disappointed man.

No longer was he the ideal man to whom she had once given all of her love. Her furrowed brow and her brusque voice told him so.

"Do we really have to go through this interrogation?" she asked him. "Are you that uncertain about the way things are between you and me?"

"I'm very certain about the way things are between us," he said. "I'm very certain that you do not love me—at least not in the same way. You've convinced yourself that you still love Ethan."

Once again, she lied to him.

"That's not so," she answered him. "I was never really in love with Ethan. My relationship with him is finished. That is the truth. There is nothing more that I need to say. Apparently, you don't want the truth. You want to be right, even if your thinking falls so wide of the mark."

"Tell me what we both know. You still love Ethan, and you are not letting him go. You're planning to team up with him again. You want him to share your bed. You want him inside you. Tell me that! Tell me because it's true!"

Now, while he kept shouting his words at her, he grabbed her by the shoulders and shook her so aggressively that the clasp of her necklace broke open. The gleaming cluster of diamonds fell across the Aubusson carpet. She tried, without avail, to pull away from him.

"Don't!" she screamed. "Don't do this to us!"

She was fighting his hold of her now. She started to punch his chest and to scratch his face with the long fingernails that she had just polished, so that they would enhance her glamorous appearance at the dinner party.

He grew even more furious because she had refused to admit that she still loved Ethan and because there had been unleashed in her defense of herself not only a rebellious spirit, but also a new contempt for him. So, he began to slap her—again and again. He hit her so hard that she might have fallen across the floor or onto the bed. But he held her tautly in front of himself, pinioning her as though she were his captive.

"Tell me the truth," he kept demanding, until his shouts had become a raspy whisper and his anger had spent itself upon his harsh slapping of her face and her upper body.

Only when he noticed that she was bleeding did he draw away from her. Only then did he lean against the bedpost. His rugged shoulders slumped as if in defeat. His entire body, with its muscular textures and well-honed powers, relaxed and appeared untypically diminished.

By then, Mrs. O'Hara, the good-hearted housekeeper, was knocking—apprehensive and importuning—on their locked door. She had heard the shouting and, perhaps, even the slaps that were like punches. She and her husband, a tall and lean cavalry officer from the First World War who, here in this sequestered place, was both a wise manager and the primary groundskeeper, had served Ryan's family for two decades and more. It was they who oversaw a staff of seven well-trained persons. The O'Haras' meticulous capacities continued to bring to the Newport estate excellent care and a renovative, aesthetic ambiance.

Mrs. O'Hara, gray-haired and motherly, called out to Ryan and her, even while she went on knocking on the door.

"Is everything all right?" she inquired. "Is there any way that I can help?"

His head bowed and his body still slumping within the masculine confines of his self-hatred, Ryan said nothing.

Still, Mrs. O'Hara knocked—this time more rapidly. The silence was a fuse to her apprehension.

She, Tracy Maguire Turner—the young wife that Mrs. O'Hara had believed enjoyed a happy marriage—hurried now to subdue the good woman's apprehension.

"It's all right, Mrs. O'Hara," she assured her. She nearly succeeded in making her voice sound natural. A smoky tremor brought a new gravity to her inflections. "Everything's all right."

After a moment, they heard Mrs. O'Hara going away.

Now Ryan left his place at the bedpost. Uncertain of what he would do next, she cautiously watched him. In her eyes, he was still a tall and impressive physicality as he stood by the French doors that he had quietly opened. The summer evening breathed its own cool vitality upon him, perhaps recognizing him as a kindred Spirit. As she watched him, she imagined that the brisk air quickened his pulse and quickened too the life of the room, touching everything in it with crisp breezes and the fragrance of blooming flowers. The glow of the moon hurried in, as well, lingering about him as though it meant to watch him.

The bracing air revived him, though (she imagined) it could not appease the shame he felt at having struck his wife. He had lost control, a sign of weakness that he would have disdained and even loathed in any man. He had failed himself and failed her. But he was going to tough it out. He would put this hour behind him and go forward.

So, she told herself even while she enjoyed the unhappiness he was experiencing. With an acute knowledge of herself, she had to admit that her need to avenge herself against his past infidelities was a dark blemish upon her conscience. She could not forgive him for his offenses. Nor could she forgive herself for her transgression. Perhaps, in ways both obvious and subtle, she would always want to punish Ryan. For herself, being with him and not with Ethan would become a lasting punishment.

From his place at the French doors, Ryan turned to face her once more. She quickly peered at him and then looked away as she seated herself before her mirror. She was not weeping, even though she had withdrawn to the bitter privacies of regret and guilt and sorrow. She was determined to pass through this hour tough-minded and pragmatic. Carefully, she willed herself to make repairs to her appearance. Her face was bruised, and her hair and her dress were disarranged. To lift her arm so that she might readjust her earrings cost her some pain. She wondered whether, as she fought against Ryan's hold of her, she had sprained her arm or even fractured it. But she did not wince in anguish or pause with uncertainty during this careful refashioning of herself. Though a discreet application of cosmetics would conceal most of the bruises his rough hand had wrought upon her face, even the most proficient make-up could not hide the swelling beneath her left eye and cheek and the lacerations upon her neck.

If their friends at the dinner party asked about her injuries, she would tell them that she had been thrown while riding an Appaloosa that was new to her.

Observing him in this moment, she saw that Ryan was aware that—with her steadfast realism and her refusal to pity herself—she had smoothly summoned her poise and whatever equally essential capacities she needed to meet the evening before her. In spite of or perhaps because of this violent confrontation between them, he continued to admire her spirit. Even now, in this hour that roiled with his angry feeling of betrayal, she was convinced that he loved her beauty, her courage, and her razor-sharp intellect. She saw the irony of their situation. Though he had been a serial adulterer, he wanted her all for himself. He could not live comfortably in a world that harbored any other man who might be her lover. She sensed, as well, another truth that was binding him to her. He did not want to lose her— at least, not yet. His wily instincts warned him that, in this complicated matter of Ethan, he must not on this evening commit himself to reprisal or to any other action. If he did, he would lose the only woman that he once believed he would love forever. Her intuition told her that, tonight, his belief in that love had faltered. No longer was he certain that they would rekindle the passionate love that had made the first year of their marriage both magical and tremendous. No longer did the excitement of falling in love with her again anchor itself to lasting happiness or to the immense experience of feeling reborn. Nevertheless, he was not yet renouncing that aspiration. He would try again. He would be a patient lover. He would prove to her that the love between a man and a woman, when it is authentic, can withstand various upheavals. That same love can anchor itself to new affirmation and new ecstasy. He would stay in this serious game that he was playing with her. His pride in his male aptitudes and his conviction that, despite her recent dallying with Ethan, she might still be capable of falling in love with him again would not permit him to follow any other path or, with her, to play any other serious game.

With these thoughts in mind (or so she imagined), Ryan crossed the room to the dressing table and mirror before which she was seated and was artfully restoring her beauty.

"I'm sorry," he said, not without genuine compunction and profound affection. "Tonight, I've been a beast. I couldn't stop myself. I didn't even want to. I had to have it out with you. I needed to clear the air of whatever it is that is preventing you from loving me as you once did."

She turned to him and, at first, said nothing. She could see how wretched he felt and how difficult it was for him to let go of his doubts. That he was making so strong an effort impressed her. On this evening, she guessed, he must have realized more than he had on any other evening that they could save their marriage only if they faced the truth together. So, she willed herself to say all the words that needed to be said.

"I began my affair with Ethan because I wanted to rouse your jealousy and because I wanted to prove to you that another man found me desirable. I hadn't imagined that I would fall in love with him. I never thought that Ethan, with his angry resentment and his distrust of almost everyone and everything, would fall in love with me. What I did learn was that, even though his love for me is ambivalent and angry and possessive and sadistic, I have found that he and I are well-matched. We are both unhappy, and we no longer regard the world as our friend. Nor can he and I be each other's safe haven. Our anger and doubts and resentments allow us no peace."

He stood silent before the mysteries of her confession. If her words disconcerted him, he allowed neither a frown nor a tight-lipped grimness to influence his regard of her. Nor did he care to choose any words that might draw him away from the quieter path he had just entered.

She hurried to say more. She used the moment to remind him once again how things were with them.

"If we are to go on together—and I intend to try very hard to make things work for us—we will have to make the best of things. We've both made mistakes. My experience with Ethan has taught me a few hard lessons. I am not sorry for the experience. Even now, I'm not certain that I want to let go of him. But I'll try to let go. I'll keep trying until he becomes a distant memory."

Still, Ryan stood near her. His rugged manliness seemed to rise over her as she sat by the mirror recomposing the imagery that her friends at the dinner party were to receive as an accurate reflection of her personhood. Still, he held himself in silence. He was not brooding and, in fact, allowed a thin smile to cross his lips. He wanted to reassure her that no new words she told him would anger him or throw him off the proper course that they must travel together.

She probed further.

"Can you forget about Ethan and me? Can you try to forgive me for having loved him, even as I am trying to forgive you for all your temporary women?"

Before her question, Ryan hesitated. He used the moment to weigh her words carefully and to calculate the number of weeks and months and possibly years they might need to forget and to forgive each other's transgressions. But even this uneasy moment passed. Then he answered her question—straightforward and matter of fact.

"I'll try very hard," he promised. "I'll work with you to make a new beginning."

Hearing his words, she felt that they had survived a crisis. Perhaps, after all, they were going to be all right together.

7

For a time, after that evening, all *was* well with them.

During the first weeks after that evening, she sensed nonetheless that, beneath their cool-headed exchanges and their well-measured reciprocal courtesies, Ryan and she still carried between them a muted enmity. Even when she was swimming with him in the heated pool within the west wing of their home or sailing with him on the sun-touched waters of a late August sea or, when—at one of the extraordinary parties that his parents hosted—he was dancing with her on the south terrace while piano and violin and trumpet played riffs upon the melodies of Cole Porter and Irving Berlin, or when he joined her and two friends in a game of tennis, they withheld themselves from each other. They held back, that is, the intimate gestures and responses that had always before—in happier times— appeared as natural as they were extemporaneous. Now, to her eyes at least, her relationship with her husband seemed contrived and rehearsed. Nor did Ryan's reactions to her anchor themselves to the casual and the authentic.

She saw in him what others could not see, because they did not know how to read the enigmatic language of his face, his voice, and his gestures. They saw and heard only surface expressions. They missed the layers of his existence. They did not perceive, as she did, the raw tension that bound him tightly to its ordinances, as though his unease was born out of anguish or despair or guilt.

His secret unhappiness, she was convinced, yoked itself to her transgression. Not only had she slept with Ethan. She had also fallen in love with him. It was her willingness to love Ethan even now, despite his murderous violence, that disgusted Ryan. Her perverse need of Ethan kept feeding Ryan's sorrow and his resentment. Of that, the pensive stillness that sometimes hovered about him and the determined smile that resisted the outward show of melancholy assured her.

Yet, in spite of his doubts of her, Ryan stayed the course that they had set for each other. He accepted the challenge. He was not yet ready to abandon his desire to win back her love. Nor was he yet ready to abandon his love for her.

Now, in mid-September, during his free time away from his busy career, he arranged private meetings and occasional excursions with her. They water-skied across the waters of Narragansett Bay, forty miles away from their Newport estate. They went skydiving from an airfield in Boston. They dined in a luxurious beach hotel in Greenwich, Connecticut. They rode palominos on a horse farm a few miles away from their home. Yet none of these excursions restored the purity or reclaimed the ecstasy of their early love. They had violated the promises of that early love. They had squandered its riches and its sustenance.

Like errant pilgrims in ancient Bible stories who had lost sight of their proper destination, she and Ryan carried their transgressions like so much heavy baggage upon their backs.

Heartsick and bitter, she wondered whether she and Ryan could ever recover their unconditional belief in each other.

Sometimes, they made love in one of the secluded cottages on their estate without being in love. Vigorous, adept, and spermatic, Ryan reveled in his possession of her. To their ambivalent copulation, she gave herself completely. No longer did they attach to their ardency any traces of sentimentality or nostalgia. Their enjoying sex with each other served a primal need and intensified their jaded awareness that they had lost, probably forever, the genuine love they had once shared.

One afternoon, she and Ryan visited an exhibit of the Symbolist prints of Edvard Munch. He was a Norwegian artist, whose last name was pronounced as Moonk and who was famous because of his portrayals of the conflicted relationships between men and women. Until the war came, Munch had often visited Ryan's father, whom he regarded as a loyal friend and an eminent collector of American, European, Asian, and African art. They had first met many years earlier when Ryan's father attended an exhibit of Munch's art in Oslo, Norway. With his father and sometimes with Ryan, Munch shared lively conversations whenever he stayed with them for a few days in their villa at Saint-Jean-Cap-Ferrat on the French Riviera. He was a white-haired rangy gentleman whose presence dominated a room. His brown eyes glowed behind wire-rimmed glasses, their quickened gaze drawing into their awareness the persons and the objects before him. Even then, when he was in his seventies, his sculptured demeanor retained a worn handsomeness. But his large, strong hands were his most memorable feature. They were hands that were inspired by a first-rate mind. During his long career, they had created thousands of prints, paintings, watercolors, and drawings, as well as hundreds of copper plates, lithographic stones, and woodblocks.

Ryan remembered fondly Munch's discussions with him and his father about his Symbolist art. For him, the very elements of the material world such as a tree, the sky, a bed, or a face were signs or correspondences of underlying moods, emotions, and ideas.

She had never met Edvard Munch. But she had studied his art when she was a student in Farmington, Connecticut.

Here in Newport, four lithographs drew her special attention. The first was called *Separation I*. Munch had printed its imagery in black on thick crème wove paper. There is evidence of lithographic crayon in the imagery, but for the most part he used brush and tusche that lent a strong calligraphic feel to the design. The narrative the canvas suggested involved the conclusion of a love affair or, perhaps, of a marriage. A young woman, slim-hipped and begowned, stands within the right side of the canvas as she looks out at the sea that nearly touches and then flows away from her. The long strands of her beautiful, light brown hair encircle a tall, dark-haired man who stands as if caught inside a dream at the right side of the canvas. Dressed in dark clothes, he stands in the dark blue shadows of the evening and near the blood-redness of flowers. He clings to the dark trunk of a tree as if that tree were connected to the universal pulse of life. By working the shadows around the man's eyes heavily, Munch transforms the face into a mask of disbelief, anguish, and bitterness. The figures in the lithograph stand separated, divided, finished with one another.

A variant lithograph entitled *Separation II* further explores Munch's theme of the dissolution of a love affair or of a marriage. In this version, strands of the light brown hair of the sullen woman waft across the chest of the grieving man.

In an even more startling rendition of this version, Munch extensively hand-colored in yellow, red, and blue, the closeup faces of the anguished, dark-haired man and the tight-lipped remoteness of the young woman.

In a fourth lithograph printed in black on wove paper, Munch portrays an equally bleak scene. The dark space of a vaguely menacing pine forest, which Munch creates from a bold application of tusche, possesses more materiality than the trees themselves. Their spindly vertical forms are merely empty areas of lithographic stone emerging from the oppressively ashen air. Against this background, the young woman stands triumphantly beside the equally young man who huddles in the lower right part of the scene. The figure of the woman, with arms raised while caressing her head, looks out defiantly at the observer. The aggressive frontality of her figure contrasts sharply with the profile rendition of the man, whose face remains hidden to the viewer. The curve of his back, rather than the contours of his unseen face, suggests his regret and his despair.

As she studied the lithographs in the company of Ryan, she became uneasy. Against her conscious will, she saw Ryan and herself in the bleak art that Munch had created. It was, she thought, uncanny that the incisive and revealing ways that Edvard Munch, an artist who had no way of knowing about Ryan's and her troubled marriage, had brought them and their travail to life in these lithographs. Yet it was not only Ryan's and her reflections in those lithographs that roused her shame and her sorrow. It was also the presence of Ryan and the influence of his body near hers, though not next to hers—here within this impressive Newport Art Museum. Suddenly, with feelings that surprised her, she was wishing that Ryan was standing closer to her as they studied Munch's art. She wanted Ryan's long body to press against her own. She wished that his blue-eyed, handsome face was touching her cheeks as though he intended to kiss her.

She thought of her resolution to maintain her emotional independence from him. She remembered her willful violation of her fidelity toward him. She also recalled his transgressions. She tried to push away her hatred of him because of his many betrayals. As swiftly as her willfulness and her hard heart allowed, she pushed away her anger and her guilt so that she could savor this special time with him.

To displace her unease, she began commenting upon Munch's print. She used her remarks to remind Ryan of her plan to remain self-determining even though she had entered an intensely romantic relationship with him.

"If I hadn't studied Edvard Munch's art at school and enjoyed many scholarly lectures about his work," she said, "I might be surprised that he is so honest about the roles that men and women inhabit when they find themselves at the end of a love affair or the end of a marriage. Few men, I think, admit the truth of their relations with women. In this print, Munch exposes the willful bitterness of the woman and the despairing vulnerability of the man. It is he who appears to lose most in the conclusion of this love affair or in the failure of a marriage. In these lithographs, the man suffers grievously. Whether his suffering drives from his pridefulness or his bad conduct, we do not know for certain. But Munch is reminding us that even strong men can suffer. None of us—men and women—walk away unscathed from the end of a love affair or the failure of a marriage."

After carefully attending her words, Ryan moved closer and took gentle hold of her hands. He was, she felt, impressed by her words that told him how much both men and women lose in their relationships with each other. If he detected the bitterness in those words, he gave no evidence. But, in spite of his controlled demeanor, she believed that he did detect her bitterness because hers was a bitterness not unlike his own.

She knew him well. He was determined to bring a hardened heart and a tough-minded willfulness to this phase of his life and to this uneasy chapter in their marriage.

"You and I know a little at least about the mistakes that men and women make with each other," he said while he continued to study her face. "Sometimes, we become fools for love or for what we think is love. Sometimes, we make ourselves prisoners of our desires. If we are lucky, we learn how to use our desires well. We learn how to accommodate ourselves effectively to our blemished lives. We no longer aim for perfection or for romantic ideals."

"Is that what is happening to us? Are we abandoning romantic ideals for momentary pleasures?"

"Time will tell," he said. "In the meantime, let's keep making an effort. Who knows? One day, we may even rediscover our ideal selves."

"What happens if we don't rediscover them?"

"We'll carry on. We'll enjoy life with one another and maybe with partners who make desire a temporary aberration."

Instantly, she grew very still. She thought of Ethan. She wondered whether her desire for him—inordinate and lingering despite her attempts to suppress it—might push her onto his path once again.

Noticing how still she had become, Ryan observed her even more carefully. He allowed another smile to crease his lips. Perhaps, because he was street-smart and knew the ambiguous workings of desire, he was reading her thoughts. He waited a moment before he offered her more words about their future.

"At any rate," he said, "I'm convinced that we'll stay together. We may even have children. We'll please our parents. We'll maintain the approval of our friends. We'll follow all the rules of our privileged class. Let's promise ourselves to elude the *Sturm und Drang*. No storm and stress for us—let's make that a promise."

"That may be a difficult promise to keep."

"We'll keep it. From now on, we'll laugh as we push our problems aside. We'll smile and party and shrug away disappointment. We'll have a hell of a good life."

"You make all of it sound exciting."

"It will be," he said. "You'll see."